HOW to be BRAVE

Daisy May Johnson

GODWINBOOKS

HENRY HOLT AND COMPANY
NEW YORK

For my parents —D. M. J.

Henry Holt and Company, *Publishers since 1866*
Henry Holt® is a registered trademark of
Macmillan Publishing Group, LLC
120 Broadway, New York, NY 10271 • mackids.com

Our books may be purchased in bulk for promotional, educational,
or business use. Please contact your local bookseller or the Macmillan
Corporate and Premium Sales Department at (800) 221-7945 ext. 5442
or by email at MacmillanSpecialMarkets@macmillan.com.

Library of Congress Control Number: 2021906633

First edition, 2021 / Designed by Trisha Previte
Printed in the United States of America by LSC Communications,
Harrisonburg, Virginia

ISBN 978-1-250-79608-0 (hardcover)

1 3 5 7 9 10 8 6 4 2

HOW TO BE BRAVE

THIS IS A STORY ABOUT THREE THINGS

1. A lot of people being very brave in very complicated times.
2. Ducks. *Mallardus Amazonica* to be precise, but you'll find out more about that side of things later. For now, just pay attention whenever that name pops up. Trust me, it'll pop up a lot. Elizabeth wanted it to pop up a lot more than it does, but Calla and I talked her out of it. You can thank me later.
3. Footnotes. I am very fond of footnotes, and nobody else ever uses them so I thought my story would have them. You might not actually know what a footnote is, so here's a demonstration.[1] Whenever you see that little number at the side of a word or at the end of a sentence, it means that I've remembered something else I want to tell you and that something is at the bottom of the page. All you have to do is go to the bottom of the page, and make sure you're reading the right numbered thing. Obviously you don't have to read the footnotes, but it's really a lot more fun if you do.

Now that I've told you all of that, we can begin.

---

1 You figured it out! Well done. Now go back up there and finish the rest of that paragraph. Off you pop. You'll be back here soon enough.

INTRODUCING ELIZABETH

Elizabeth North is the first person you have to be introduced to. Of course there are other people in this book, and you shall meet them at the right time, but for now there is Elizabeth, for without Elizabeth there would not be a story at all. Elizabeth was a doctor. She was not one of those doctors who went around and helped people to get better. She was a very different kind of doctor—the type of doctor who knows an awful lot of things about one subject in particular, but very little about medicines or broken bones.

And the particular thing that Elizabeth knew a lot about was ducks.

Elizabeth could tell you what a duck meant when it quacked at you, why you shouldn't feed a wild duck bread,[2] why mallards are horrible fathers,[3] why ducks have such big feet,[4] and what is the best joke about ducks.[5]

. . . .

2 Bread makes their stomachs swell up.
3 I don't want to give you details but trust me, they would not get a Father's Day card from any of their children.
4 All the better to see you with, my dear.
5 Did you hear about the duck who thought he was a squirrel? He was a tough nut to quack.

She also knew a lot about how to survive, but we shall come to this later. Elizabeth had a daughter, Calla Rose,[6] a girl with bright yellow hair and three freckles that resembled the precise outline of a mallard's tertial feather, and it was just the two of them against the world. In the brief moments she could think clearly enough to work, Elizabeth did it in the only way she knew how. She wrote articles and books and sold the clothes off her own back, and kept the two of them together and afloat and alive.

It was not an easy life, and it was often one that took them away from the world. On the rare times that Elizabeth spoke to people, or that people spoke to her, they would think of her as a strange and eccentric woman and never talk to her again. Those people were—are—idiots.

Elizabeth North was one of the bravest and strongest women in the entire world.

And I am going to tell you why.

---

6 Calla comes to play quite a substantial part in this story, but right now we must stay with Elizabeth. Trust me on this.

A TEMPORARILY WONDERFUL CHILDHOOD

The young Elizabeth lived with her parents in a big house in the countryside. Although she was an only child, she did not grow up alone. She had a dog that was so large and brown, he really was more lion than dog. His name was Aslan and when Elizabeth went to school, he would sit quietly at the front door and not move until he saw her coming back up the drive.

Elizabeth's parents spoiled her deliberately and happily. They lived for the moment and her childhood was as perfectly formed as the diamonds on her mum's wedding ring. She would have chocolate cake for breakfast and ice cream for lunch before going to bed at midnight and watching fireworks outside the window. And on the days when there were no fireworks and just the distant pink of a setting sun, Elizabeth would sit outside and think about how much she loved her life. It was a strange thing for a child to think, but Elizabeth North was a strange child who lived a strange life.

She went to school, of course, and mixed with other children, but the school was down in the village and not the sort of school that you and I might even recognize as a school. It was two rooms, and the older children sat in one, and the younger children sat in the other, and Elizabeth was sent between the two rooms because there was nobody else her age. Sometimes when she was sent from one room to the other, she would wander outside instead and feed the birds with the spare crumbs from her pockets.

On one Friday in July, when it was almost the end of term and everybody was thinking about the school holidays, the little ones had been allowed to do coloring but the older ones had had to do math. Elizabeth didn't want to do either, so she was on her way to slip outside. She had gone precisely three steps when Mrs. Fraser, her tall and sensible teacher, stopped her. "Math," said Mrs. Fraser. "You need to brush up on your times tables."

"But that's not fair," said Elizabeth, folding her arms.

Mrs. Fraser didn't look concerned in the slightest.[7] "Life isn't fair, Elizabeth. You'll be doing math this afternoon and if you continue with this attitude, you'll be staying behind and doing extra. I am quite happy to do my knitting while you do some more sums. I imagine it will be educational for us both."

"You have no jurisdiction[8] on me after school," said Elizabeth.

It was somewhat inevitable that Mrs. Fraser thought the opposite.

She kept Elizabeth in detention that very day and, straight

....

7 Mrs. Fraser was EXCELLENT at appearing Unconcerned, and I think we can all learn something from her.

8 This is a fancy word that means "authority." Elizabeth had learned it only two days ago, after hearing it on the TV, and felt that this was the perfect time to practice it.

after the last little one had been picked up by their parents, spent the next hour drilling Elizabeth on why X+Y=Z. In all honesty it wasn't a very productive session because Elizabeth did not want to be there, and neither did Mrs. Fraser. [9]

But then everything changed.

---

[9] She might be a teacher, but she was still human. Just.

HOW IT HAPPENED

It began with a telephone call. It was the sort of telephone call that made Mrs. Fraser purse her lips and leave the room. She was gone for a delightfully long time during which Elizabeth took the opportunity to put her pen down, stare out the window, and consider how much she hated math. Sometimes our happiest moments come before our saddest, and Elizabeth North was no exception. She was not doing math. She was sitting in the sunshine. She was by herself. It was perfect.

The moment that followed it, however, was not.

Mrs. Fraser came back into the room. She had her hand across her mouth, as though she was trying to yawn and hide it. She stood in the doorway for a moment, before walking into the room, and even then she didn't look directly at Elizabeth. Her eyes went to the desk, the window, before coming to rest on Elizabeth's knees.

Elizabeth wriggled with discomfort. She couldn't help it.

"Elizabeth," said Mrs. Fraser to the girl's knees, "we're finished for today. I'm going to drive you home."

I suspect that if Elizabeth had been told there and then about what had happened things would have been a lot easier for everyone. But some people do not know what to do when they are presented with the unexpected, and Mrs. Fraser was one of those people. Her way of coping was to talk to Elizabeth's knees and to drive her home in silence and then to send her to her room.

"But it's not bedtime," said Elizabeth. This was a very reasonable point to make and one which was made very reasonably even though Elizabeth's stomach was starting to knot together with a strange other feeling that she thought might possibly be fear.

Mrs. Fraser looked at the front door, the carpet, and the bottom of the stairs. "I need to use your telephone to make some calls. Can you tell me where it is?"

"It's just there," said Elizabeth. A shadow in the corner of the hall shifted when she spoke. It was Aslan, and he looked as confused as Elizabeth felt. He padded his way across the floor and pushed his head into Elizabeth's hands, as though he was trying to convince himself that she was really there.

"I just need to make some calls," said Mrs. Fraser again.

"Is everything all right?" said Elizabeth. She wrapped her fingers in her dog's thick brown fur, taking comfort from his presence.

"I just need you to be brave for me now, please."

Elizabeth nodded. She nodded because she knew that was what Mrs. Fraser wanted her to do, but she was full of questions. She wanted to know what she should be brave about, she wanted to know where her parents were, and she wanted to know exactly who Mrs. Fraser was telephoning and what she was doing in her house.

But she did not say any of this because Mrs. Fraser was already walking toward the telephone and her shoulders were saying, as clearly as shoulders can say this sort of thing, that she should not be followed.

However, they were not saying that she should not be listened to.[10]

Elizabeth climbed the stairs with Aslan at her side, and when they reached the top step she sat down and so did he. She pushed her fingers under his collar, and he inched closer to her and the two of them listened with all their might to what Mrs. Fraser was saying on the phone. I do not think either of them breathed. It was that sort of a moment.

----

10 Under normal circumstances you should not listen to somebody on the phone. Their business is not your business, even if they are talking about interesting and scandalous things. However, there was a teacher in Elizabeth's house, and that was a most unusual circumstance, so Elizabeth decided that *normal* did not apply.

WHAT MRS. FRASER SAID

"Both of them? But—how?"

There was a long, awful pause before she spoke again.

"Social services . . . seriously? . . . But what on earth do I tell her?"

And thoughts—terrible, big, and almost incomprehensible thoughts—began to make themselves known inside Elizabeth's heart.

"How do I say that?" said Mrs. Fraser. She was talking so quietly that Elizabeth and Aslan had to move down a couple of steps to make sure that they could hear. "Does she not have a guardian? I can't do this by myself."

The next sentence, however, was not the sort of sentence that went unheard. It was so loud and clear that the words practically walked up the stairs and introduced themselves. "Elizabeth has no other relatives, so where on earth is she meant to go?"

Elizabeth sat very still.

"I can't tell her that her parents are dead," said Mrs. Fraser. "How can you ask me to do that?"

But it was too late. Despite her protestations that she did not know how, or even if she could, Mrs. Fraser had just told Elizabeth North that both her parents had died.

Yes.

I know.

AFTER THE END OF THE WORLD

Nothing but silence could follow such a moment, and Elizabeth took a strange sort of comfort in it. Silence was simple and straightforward because it meant that she did not have to deal with the sadness inside her heart.

And so her days became long and dark and all the same. Her mornings blurred into evenings, and midnight became midday, and all the while Elizabeth lay in her room and did not go back to school. She did not go anywhere. She stayed upstairs in her lonely house and let Mrs. Fraser take charge of everything. Sometimes Elizabeth would hear her talk to people downstairs, but as these people were not her parents and never would be, she did not let herself think about them.

In many ways, I do not think that she let herself think at all.

She simply slept and ate and ate and slept and Aslan stayed at her side throughout it all until one morning when he was not there.

And a woman was instead.

THE WOMAN WHO LOOKED A LITTLE BIT LIKE A PENGUIN

She was tall and pale and wore a long black dress that ran all the way from her neck down to her toes. She wore a white scarf wrapped around her head, and a pair of thick black spectacles that balanced on the edge of her nose. It was an overly dramatic sort of outfit, really, but befitting of overly dramatic circumstances such as these.

"Hello, Elizabeth," said the woman. "I'm a nun. Do you know what that is? I imagine you might not. Not everybody does these days. We're a bit of a dying art. We look a bit like penguins. But we're not."

This was not, perhaps, the best of openings. Allow me to elaborate. The woman's name was Good Sister June,[11] and she had been a nun for six whole months.[12] She was part of the Order[13] of the Good Sisters, a group of women who were to

---

11 This is the point where I reward you for paying attention to the footnotes. Are you ready? Okay. Here is the great secret about Good Sister June. She is me. Don't tell anybody!

12 She was so very, very new.

13 An order is simply a very posh and nun-ish way of saying "club." Nuns are very good at making things sound more complicated than they are, trust me.

become very important in Elizabeth's life. Of course Elizabeth did not know any of this, because she could not see into the future. She simply knew that her dog was nowhere to be found, and an absent dog was the sort of thing that needed to be dealt with first. When she had Aslan at her side once more, she could then figure out who this remarkably strange woman was.

"Where's my dog?" said Elizabeth.

The woman looked at the ceiling and at the curtains and at the floor, and then at the door. When she eventually replied, she looked at Elizabeth's toes.

"I knew your mother," she said.

Which was not, thought Elizabeth, anything approaching a reply.

"My name's Good Sister June. I teach at a school. Your mum came to visit us a few months ago. She was one of our pupils, back when she was a child. Did you know that?"

Elizabeth did not.

"It was lovely to see her again."

"I didn't know she was religious," said Elizabeth.

Good Sister June shrugged. "Who's to say what 'religious' is?"

"You're a nun," said Elizabeth. "Isn't that what you do? Isn't it your job?"

"No," said Good Sister June, and for the first time since she'd entered the room, she sounded confident. She had even begun to talk to Elizabeth's face, and that was something that no other adult had been able to do since the day that *it* had happened. "We do have a bit of religion, but my order doesn't actually believe in God. Not in the way that a lot of other people do. We believe in education and trying to do the right thing and, basically, helping other people be the best they can be. We run a school, and some of us pray in private, and some of us work in the community."

"Brilliant," said Elizabeth.

It was not the sort of *brilliant* that meant "brilliant" at all. Good Sister June knew this, which is why she looked away from Elizabeth's face and directed the next sentence to her left ankle. "But when your mum came to see us, she didn't come to talk about that. She came to talk to us about you. She knew that you had no other family and so, in the case that something . . . something happened either to her or her husband—your father—she wanted to make sure that you were safe. It's rather wonderful that she did."

Elizabeth did not think there was anything wonderful about any of this.

"I want my dog."

Good Sister June nodded. "I'm quite sure you do. But I just need you to understand what I'm saying. Your mother asked me to be your guardian and I accepted. Do you know what that means?"

"It means you'll look after me and Aslan," said Elizabeth. "Where is he?"

"He's downstairs—"

"Why isn't he here?"

"Elizabeth, I promise you, he's fine and you'll be able to see him in a moment but I need you to listen to what I'm telling you. You're going to come with me and live in our school. It's a boarding school, so that means there will be other girls there too. It's a nice setup. You'll be sleeping in one of the tower bedrooms, I think. The school is surrounded by trees but you can see beyond them from the towers. I think if you were to stand on the roof there, you could probably see for miles. Maybe even all the way to the sea."

"I'm not going anywhere," Elizabeth said bluntly. "I'm going to stay here with my dog."

"I'm afraid you can't," said Good Sister June, gently.

The two of them stared at each other.

"You're too young," said Good Sister June. "Social services won't let you grow up here by yourself. They want the best for you, and so did your parents. That means school. At least until you're eighteen. That's when you'll come into your inheritance, and be able to make your own choices. But until then, it's us. There's no other option. I promise you it's not that bad. You'll make friends your own age, and we don't do lessons all the time. Quite the opposite, in fact. It's never been that sort of an establishment. We bake buns and go for walks and it's like a little family. Normally we meet pupils off the train at the start of term, but I'll drive us straight there under the circumstances. Give you a guided tour."

And then Good Sister June took a deep breath and said the awful thing: "You can't bring the dog."

A small sound of pain escaped Elizabeth's throat.

"We can't have pets. I'm so sorry, Elizabeth, but we just can't. There's no room. Aslan is a big dog and he needs space to run around and play, and we just don't have the facilities for that at the school. There's barely enough room for us as it is. Mrs. Fraser is going to take him. She'll look after him,

Elizabeth. She has such a big garden. She can give him the care he needs. You don't have to say goodbye. Not until you're ready. And not forever. She's going to send you updates on him. That is, if you'd like them. We'll do this your way, Elizabeth, there's no rush. We're not going anywhere until you're okay with that."

Somehow Elizabeth found her voice then. It was not her old, familiar voice, but it was one that would do for the moment and she was not sure that she could manage anything else.

"It's okay," she said, even though it was not. She looked toward the door, knowing that Aslan lay beyond it and that she could not say goodbye to him even if she tried.

There was nothing else to be done.

"I don't want to stay here a moment longer," she said. "I want to go now."

AT THE SCHOOL OF THE GOOD SISTERS

Though she did not expect it, nor even want it, Elizabeth North came to love that school with all of her heart. She would not have sent her only daughter there if she had not. When you do not have many people in the world that you love, you take a lot of care of the ones that you have. And Calla Rose was all that Elizabeth had.

But I'm getting a bit ahead of myself.

Calla's story will be told shortly, I promise, but for now, we must stay with Elizabeth and the School of the Good Sisters. Her first few weeks there did not go well. She spent her days surrounded by people, but was for all intents and purposes alone. It was grief that made her this way, and it was natural to be like this, for she had experienced something awful, but there had to be an end to it. There had to be a point where her grief would stop and Elizabeth would come back to the world.

And then on one bright Sunday, as the children came home from church after paying tribute to a faith that half of them couldn't pronounce and a service the other half slept through, something happened that did precisely that.

That something was a small brown duck.[14] It was sitting in the road, with the expression of somebody who didn't quite know how they'd ended up there, and its wing was held at a strange and sharp angle. Chrissie Poplin was the first to see it and so she said "There's a duck sat in the road!" and looked around to see if everybody had noticed what was happening.

"There is a duck *sitting* in the road," said Good Sister Robin, who was a stickler for good grammar.[15]

The prim line of children ignored her. They were too busy scattering and running over to where Chrissie stood. Good Sister June swept along with the children as though she were leading them into battle, until she raised her hand and halted everyone a few meters away from the duck. She said, "If anyone—and I am looking at you, Magda DeWitt[16]—goes one step nearer to that poor, terrified creature without my permission, I will send them to bed early for a week."

And every child, including Magda DeWitt and Chrissie Poplin, stopped dead where they were.

Every child, that is, except Elizabeth North.

....

14 Are you sensing a theme here? Good. I knew you were smart.

15 She is very lovely, but we do all have our faults.

16 Magda DeWitt is a name that is very important to this story, and I'd like to tell you a little bit about her. She was the sort of girl who did not make sense in buildings: She could only breathe properly in the open fields and under a bright blue sky. She was smart: madly, furiously so, but this was not an easy sort of knowledge for her to have inside of herself. She could not control it easily. She was the sort of girl that some people might have simply called naughty or bad. But Magda was never simple nor straightforward, and the people who thought she was were fools.

INTRODUCING DUCKS

Elizabeth moved forward and when Good Sister June turned around to tell her off, she found herself falling silent instead. The girl knelt down and cupped her hand around the duck. She was holding it so gently that it might have been a baby, whilst whispering something under her breath. When she realized that Good Sister June was watching her, she gave the nun a quick, half-shy look and said, "The wing is broken. If I splint it, it'll heal and the duck can fly again."

"Do you even know what a splint is?" asked Good Sister June. She did not mean to sound disbelieving, but she had not heard Elizabeth speak voluntarily for months now. The fact that she had suddenly become proficient in first aid for ducks was really quite difficult to come to terms with.

Elizabeth nodded. "It's a support to help the bone heal. I can strap it up. I know how. I watched my dad do it once."

Good Sister June waved her hand at Good Sister Robin. "Take the girls home," she said. "We'll catch up with you."

When Good Sister Robin had bustled all of the children away, murmuring sweet nothings about adverbs and proper nouns, Good Sister June lifted up her habit[17] and knelt down on the road beside Elizabeth. She looked at the girl and chose her next words very carefully. "It looks pretty badly hurt. I need you to understand what that means. This might not work. Besides, if it's a wild duck, then it won't be used to having humans around at all and the stress of that might be too much for it to handle."

Elizabeth didn't reply. Instead, she slowly teased out the wing of the bird and let her fingers work out where the break was. The small brown duck closed its eyes. For an awful moment Good Sister June thought it had died but then she saw its chest start to move up and down and realized that the girl had, of all things, sent it to sleep.

As though in a dream, Elizabeth said, "I tried to remember my dad's face today and I couldn't. I could remember that he had brown hair and brown eyes but I couldn't remember him. How he looked. How he was. I thought maybe it was just him that I'd forgotten, but I couldn't—it was the same with my mum. I couldn't remember either of them. It's as if they weren't ever there at all." Her fingers stopped moving and she nodded to herself with satisfaction. "There, I found it. It's a straight break. I think I can help it. Will you find me a stick? I need something really small but really strong."

Good Sister June glanced around her and then inspiration hit. All of the nuns wore their hair pinned back under their scarves so that it wasn't visible. "Would a hair clip do?" she said, obedient to the odd authority in Elizabeth's voice. She worked one of

---

17 A habit is a special type of dress. Nuns have special words for everything.

her clips free and dropped it into Elizabeth's outstretched hand. The girl began to bend out the metal so that it formed a smooth line and laid it over the curve of the duck's wing. She took her handkerchief out of her pocket, placed the corner of it between her teeth, and tore a thin strip off. She used this to bind the clip into place before flexing the wing very gently to make sure that it would all stay in place. And somehow, the duck slept through the entire procedure.

"I know how to do this," said Elizabeth. "One of the swans on the lake got hurt once, and my dad splinted its wing, and I don't understand how I can remember all of that like it was yesterday but I can't even remember his face."

There was nothing that Good Sister June could say.

Elizabeth got carefully to her feet, cradling the duck against her chest. She said, "I know that it might die. And if it does, it does, but I have to try to make it better. Please let me. It needs a chance."

"We don't allow pets, you know this. I'm sorry, Elizabeth, but I can't make exceptions." Elizabeth opened her mouth to protest but Good Sister June held up her hand and stopped her, quite firmly. "We do, however, allow patients," she said, "and I will allow you to bring this duck home. I will make arrangements for you to have a private space outside to nurse it back to health. You will release it once it is fit and healthy. Are we agreed?"

Elizabeth nodded. "Yes," she said. A small smile crept across her face. "Thank you."

THE FIRST FRIEND
OF ELIZABETH NORTH

Elizabeth brought the duck with the broken wing back to full health the same way that people wake up in the morning and go to bed at night. There was simply no option for the duck other than to get better, and so it did. When the evenings grew warm, she went outside and fed it rolled oats[18] from the palm of her hand and told it that it would be well. As the duck ate, she ran her fingers softly along its bones and felt them knitting back into position. She removed the splint after two weeks, and after another had passed, she knew that the duck was ready to be released back into the world.

But she also knew that she didn't want to let it go.

It was an understandable sentiment for anyone, and perhaps for Elizabeth North, who had lost everything and everyone she held dear, even more so.

She wrestled with these thoughts for a long, long time, and the only thing that distracted her was the wonder of the duck

---

18 You might be asking why she fed it rolled oats and not bread. The fact is that Elizabeth was starting to learn about ducks and one of the first things she had learned was that bread was not very good for ducks. Rolled oats, corn, and seeds were much better things.

itself. She was fascinated by the way its neck could twist and stretch so far across its body, and the quick, sharp movements of its beak as it cleaned its feathers. Sometimes when she watched it, she would read from a book about ducks that she'd found in the library and name parts of it as though she were casting a spell: *calamus, umbilicus, rachis, vane.*

It was perhaps unsurprising that the duck did not answer her during these moments. However, a girl who had been pretending to weed the communal vegetable patch in the schoolyard did. This was Chrissie Poplin, the girl who had first spotted the duck back on that Sunday morning all those weeks ago, and she had taken a special interest in the situation ever since. She had not wished to actually touch the duck,[19] but she was quite interested in it nonetheless, as it was something different. The fact that it had gotten Elizabeth out of the evening lectures from Good Sister Honey on light aircraft maintenance was not on her mind in the slightest.[20]

Chrissie said, "Is your duck getting better?"

"Yes," said Elizabeth. She was watching the duck lift up each wing to preen the feathers underneath. She found the duck much more interesting than anything else at the school and so a part of her was not surprised when Chrissie sat down beside her. Remembering the way that she'd yelled about the duck back when they first saw it, Elizabeth said, "You can stay but you have to talk quietly. It gets scared."

....

19 Chrissie Poplin was one of those girls who was suspicious of things that she had not directly experienced. Thus ducks, olives, and Latvia all featured on the same and rather eccentric list.

20 It was. Nobody liked those lectures.

Chrissie nodded and watched the way the duck continued to ruffle through its feathers as though neither of them were there. "Is this what you did back in your house? Before you came here?"

Chrissie knew Elizabeth's story. They all did. It was like something out of a book by Eva Ibbotson, and as books by Eva Ibbotson and others like her were among their favorite books from the school library's well-used collection, the whole school had devoured the real-life tragedy that Elizabeth North had given them.

Elizabeth shook her head. "Not really," she said. "I just knew what to do. I mean, when I saw that it had a broken bone."

"It's pretty cool, though. You fixed it. You made him better."

Elizabeth realized suddenly that she'd never thought of the duck as having a gender. It had simply been a duck. It. That. "Him?" she said, looking at the duck as though it was the first time she'd ever seen it. "Do you think it's a boy?"

"Definitely," Chrissie said, with a confidence that denied the fact that she was failing biology that term. She reached out her hand, unable to stop herself, and carefully touched the very tip of the nearest feather. It felt oily and strangely thick. "I thought it'd be lighter," she said. "It must be really heavy to have to carry them all the time."

"Those feathers have to deal with a lot. He can't put a coat on if it gets rainy. Or a scarf when it gets cold."

"You should be a vet," said Chrissie. "When you leave here, I mean."

Elizabeth shook her head. "I couldn't do the gross bits. But maybe, I don't know, I could do something else with animals.

I like finding out things about them. It makes you understand them better."

"I want to teach," said Chrissie. "Maybe I'll even come back and teach here. I want to be the cool teacher that everyone remembers."

"If I was in your class, I'd remember you."

Chrissie did not believe in false modesty. She nodded in approval of Elizabeth's assessment and said, "Yes, you would. So can we be friends?"

"Yes," said Elizabeth. "All right."

And then the two of them looked at each other and realized that they were friends and that they would be friends for the rest of their lives.

After all of the complicated things that had happened in Elizabeth's life, it really was just as simple as that.

THE VALUE OF A VERY GOOD LIBRARY IN TIMES OF NEED

And so a small brown duck and the bright and fierce friendship of Chrissie Poplin brought Elizabeth back to the world. She would bicker and joke and laugh with Chrissie for hours and hours, and when she felt sad, she would go and hide in the library and manage all of her grief in a way that she had not been able to do before.

The library was the perfect space for this sort of thing. It was a long room with windows that stretched all the way from the floor to the ceiling, and just enough shelves to allow somebody to have a little cry behind one of them. There were not, however, enough shelves for the books. They were piled two or three deep on most, and where they didn't fit on the shelves, they rose in towers from the floor. Sometimes if you did not know where the shelves started and the walls ended, it could look as if the whole room was built from books. It was also a space that held secrets, and Elizabeth had discovered some of them. She had found her favorite seat, for example, tucked away in a secret corner past Frances Hodgson Burnett and Noel Streatfeild. It was right next to a window and sometimes, when the light was just right, she could see all the way out into the wood.[21]

And one day, when Elizabeth was sitting there, recovering from her memories and the persistent ache of her sadness, something most peculiar happened.

---

21 She had not discovered, however, one of my favorite secrets, which was the cake tub located just behind Angela Brazil and filled to the brim with slices of sticky and delicious parkin.

THE OTHER PERSON IN THE LIBRARY

Magda DeWitt appeared from around the back of the shelves. Her hair was a mess and her eyes were suspiciously red. Elizabeth was the sort of person who knew what it meant when people looked like that and so, when Magda stared at her and said, "What are you doing here?" in an *I've definitely not been crying* sort of voice, Elizabeth could not stop herself.

"Have you been crying?" she asked with interest. You may not be surprised to discover that Magda did not answer her question. I do not think that many people would have answered, but Elizabeth was still discovering what sorts of things were appropriate to say to other people.

"Shut up," said Magda. "Why are you here?"

Elizabeth gestured at her notebook and said, "I'm studying." She had made it a habit to take some work into the library every time she went. It acted as a useful cover story. It was the sort of tip that she would have given other people in similar circumstances, but Magda was not other people.

Magda folded her arms. "I don't believe it. You haven't opened the book."

She had a point. It was a point, however, that Elizabeth was not willing to concede. "I was thinking," she said. "And then I'll write. Why does it matter to you anyway?"

"You can't do that here."

"What?" Elizabeth said blankly. She was growing increasingly confused by the whole conversation. "Loads of people come in here."

"No," said Magda. "This is my thing."

"What's your thing?"

Magda stared at her. "I sit here. This is *my* seat. I sit here and I do my homework and I get good marks. You've stolen everything from me. I'm not having you steal this as well."

"I literally don't have a clue what you're on about," said Elizabeth.

Magda rolled her eyes. "Chrissie."

"What does she have to do with this?"

"She was my friend. We'd been friends for years before you came. But now she's your friend instead. *And* you're helping her get better marks. I bet you've been helping her with her homework. This is a plot between the two of you."

"You and Chrissie haven't been friends for years. Trust me, I know all about it,"[22] said Elizabeth. "And, look, I'm not helping her with her homework. Why would I? She could get better

----

22 This was true. Chrissie and Magda had in fact been friends for precisely two days in their very first year at school, until Magda had insisted on helping herself to Chrissie's slice of chocolate cake without asking. Taking anything without asking is a very bad decision and taking cake without permission is a very, very bad decision. From that day, Chrissie had decided to make friends with people who understood the value of cake. Magda, as you can see, was still trying to come to terms with the entire affair.

marks than you with her eyes closed. Both of us could. Half the class could."[23]

"I'd like to see you try. I've been the head of the class for years now, and that's not going to change now you're here."

"And yet you can't figure out why you don't have any friends."

"Your best friend's a duck," said Magda.

"Newborn ducks understand abstract thoughts," said Elizabeth, and then she took pity on Magda because she really was looking quite upset about it all, and elaborated, "You wouldn't think it, but baby ducks are actually very smart. It's a thing called 'relational matching'—"

Magda held up her hand. "I know about ducks."

"You totally don't."

"I will," Magda said grimly. "If it takes doing a project about ducks, then I'll do that. I'll make it better than yours. Better than anything you could ever do." She reached over the desk and grabbed the notebook before Elizabeth could react. Flicking through the first few pages, she pulled a face. "'Nesting habits of ducks in the Amazon.' Fine. All right. I'm going to submit this as my own work. They'll believe it's mine. Why would the smartest girl in the school copy from somebody else?"

Elizabeth stared at her. "We've never even spoken to each other, and this is the first thing you want to do? Steal my work and get better marks?"

....

23 This went down as well as you might have expected.

"Yes," said Magda. "You can't stop me. You've stolen everything from me. Now you're going to know how it feels."

But before Magda had even finished speaking, Elizabeth had grabbed the notebook back. She picked up her pen and began to scribble over everything she'd written, and it was only when the paper was more black than white that Elizabeth let it go. "Hand that in," she said, and she could not help herself from feeling very smug when she did so. "Go on. I hope you get great marks. I think they might comment on your presentation skills, though."

Magda said something very rude[24] before she placed her hands on her hips. "This isn't over. You can't keep an eye on that book forever. I'll get it from you somehow, and I'll steal your work. I'll steal everything from you."

And then, because she really did have a flair for the dramatic, she spun on her heels and stormed out of the library.

Elizabeth took a deep breath and sat back down beside a pile of E. Nesbits. She had a problem to solve. The problem wasn't about wondering how Magda was going to steal her notebook; it was about figuring out what to do when she did. Magda seemed to be the sort of person who carried out her threats, and that meant that Elizabeth had to deal with this in a different fashion or deal with her homework being stolen from her for the rest of her life.

But Magda had made one mistake about Elizabeth North, and it was one that would have a greater ramification than

---

24 No, I won't tell you what it was. Not even if you bribe me with a slice of lemon drizzle.

either of them could ever have imagined. Elizabeth was a survivor. She had survived the loss of her parents, her dog, and her home. She had survived the loss of the life that she had lived. She had survived the loss of chocolate cake for breakfast and ice cream for supper and a home full of love and laughter.

She had survived worse than Magda DeWitt, and she would continue to do so all her life.

As she sat there, Elizabeth came to a realization. Her work could only be stolen if it could be read, and that meant that all she had to do was write it in a way Magda wouldn't understand. Magda was famed throughout the school for her obsession with learning new languages, so writing it in something like French or Spanish wasn't an option. Elizabeth also didn't want to spend the rest of her time at school scribbling over all of her notes, so that wasn't an option, either.

Code, however, was.

She would write everything out in code and then rewrite it just before she had to hand it in. It would be extra work,[25] sure, but Magda wouldn't be able to read one bit of it.

Elizabeth pulled out the page that she'd scribbled over and began a new one, figuring out the code as she went along. She was smiling.

---

[25] Sometimes there is "extra work" that involves things like multiplying Brussels sprouts with cabbage and thus is the worst thing ever. Sometimes there is "extra work" that feels a little bit like a firework in your heart. Writing in code was a firework for Elizabeth, and she could not wait to get started.

RAINBOW SPONGE AND CHOCOLATE CUSTARD

It was a rainy day when the next phase of Elizabeth and Magda's relationship began. They were hiding from the weather in their common room, along with all of the other girls in their year. There were a lot of girls and not much room; girls sat on chairs and on lockers and on the floor, and all of them were suffering from the peculiar sensation that is rainy day boredom.

Elizabeth and Chrissie pulled some cushions into the corner and started a long, lazy and comfortable argument over the best desserts. "Rainbow sponge and chocolate custard," Chrissie said confidently, for it was the sort of discussion that required confident statements. "Good Sister Robin made it for lunch once and it was the absolute best and she's never made it again, and I miss it literally every day."

"I don't believe Good Sister Robin even knows what custard looks like."[26]

"She did, she made it, and it wa—"

"I don't believe you," Elizabeth said with a grin. She dodged

----

26 She does a mean roly-poly with custard now, let me tell you that.

the cushion that Chrissie threw at her, and then threw it back. Elizabeth was good at many things, but she was not that good at throwing, and instead of hitting Chrissie, the cushion smashed into the head of the person who had been sitting with her back to them. And that person was Magda DeWitt.

Magda turned round, furious. "Stop it!"

"Stop what?" said Chrissie.

"Throwing things. And you're being so loud. Just shut up. I'm trying to concentrate."

"There's twenty-three other girls in here. Why aren't you telling them to shut up?"

"I'm telling *you*. You have to be quiet in here."

"That's not a rule," said Chrissie with some justification.[27] "And we're not being noisy, Magda, we're just being normal. You should try it sometime." Some of the other girls in the room had started to listen in. A couple of them laughed out loud at this.

"You don't understand. I need to finish my homework."

Chrissie raised her eyebrows. "Haven't you copied it from Elizabeth recently?"

"Oh my god, Magda, is that your new thing?" said one of the girls who was listening.[28] She pulled a face of disgust. "Nobody normal thinks like that."

- -

27 Having broken many of the rules at school, she was innately familiar with them.

28 This was Penelope Mortimer, and once upon a time, Magda had helped herself to Penelope's chips without asking.

"Just for once, can't you be like everybody else?" said another girl.[29] "Stop being so mean."

A strange feeling of sympathy suddenly rose inside of Elizabeth. She knew full well that Magda had been trying to crack the code in her notebook and failing. The book kept disappearing and reappearing on her desk, and Magda kept turning in work that had clearly been done at the last minute on a completely different topic. Her grades were going down. She couldn't be happy with how things were working out.

"Magda," Elizabeth said quietly, ignoring the shrieks of laughter around them, "I'm sorry I threw the cushion at you. I didn't mean to, I promise."

Magda glared at her. "You meant it. You always do—"

"I'm apologizing," said Elizabeth. "It's up to you if you want to accept it." She turned to Chrissie. "Will you come with me? I want to go and talk to Good Sister June, and now seems like a perfect time."

"Are you telling her about me?" said Magda.

"Please," said Elizabeth with spectacular disdain. "I have better things to do."

And she did. She waited until they were halfway down a deserted corridor before she pulled Chrissie to the side and said, "I'm going to release the duck tonight. It's the right weather, and I think it's the right time."

---

29 This was Jasmine Swann, and once upon a time, Magda had helped herself to Jasmine's crayons without asking. You may be sensing a theme here with Magda helping herself to things she did not own. You would be right.

Chrissie looked appalled. "You're going to send him out into this? It's been raining for like the past four years."

"He's *Mallardus Amazonica.* I don't know how he ended up in England, but he's actually from the Amazon rainforest. Rain is his best friend. This is the best day I could ever do it. Anyway, he should be migrating now and I don't want him to miss it."

"But what's that got to do with Good Sister June?"

"I want her there," said Elizabeth. She didn't look at Chrissie. "I want you both there. I think it has to be the three of us. Nobody else. He needs to be sent off today and that's the way I want to do it."

"Okay," said Chrissie slowly, at last figuring out why she'd been dragged away from a perfectly promising argument with her nemesis. "Do I have to hold him?"

"No, you don't."

"Good."

"Will you come?"

"You know I will."

And when they reached Good Sister June's office and explained the situation to her, that was exactly what the nun said. Admittedly she said it in more teacherly English,[30] but the intent was still the same. The three of them would meet in the yard at five o'clock, release the duck, and be back just in time for supper.[31]

. . . .

30 "I will join you for this endeavor, Elizabeth, and I'm grateful to you for the invitation."

31 Everything should be done in time for supper. It's the best meal of the day. The second best, by the way, is afternoon tea. I am very fond of a good scone.

A FEW WORDS ABOUT MAGDA DEWITT

I imagine that you've been annoyed by somebody in your life. People can be very annoying, it's true. I myself suffer constant vexation at the acts of others. Good Sister Honey, for example, has a deplorable tendency to put jam in a chocolate cake.[32]

Magda and Elizabeth[33] were like chocolate and jam; they did not go together in the slightest. Elizabeth could cope with this because she had Chrissie to talk to, but Magda didn't have a best friend. She didn't have any friends at all, and ever since Elizabeth had arrived, she had not been the best version of herself. Much of this is because she wanted to be friends with Elizabeth and couldn't bring herself to admit it, let alone figure out how to make it happen. But then, these are not the easiest things to realize when you are chocolate and everything else around you is jam.

It might not surprise you to learn that Magda followed Elizabeth and Chrissie out of the common room on that rainy

---

32 I'm grateful for the cake, of course, but I'm also rather appalled that she thinks chocolate and jam is a legitimate combination when they do not go together under any circumstances.

33 And to be fair, Magda and the rest of the world.

day. She had listened to them talk about the duck and then listened to them talk to Good Sister June, and after all of that, she had hidden until the coast was clear and then gone outside to the little yard where the duck lived.

I do not know what she was going to do when she got there, but I can tell you this.

I am very glad that she ran into Good Sister June before she did it.

AN ENEMY IS FOR LIFE, NOT JUST FOR CHRISTMAS

"Hello, Magda. Are you going somewhere? You do know it's still raining?" Magda let out a tiny little shriek of surprise.

"I'm not sure that's a valid response," said Good Sister June, who was, I think, enjoying the encounter a little bit too much. "You shouldn't be out here. Not when Good Sister Robin's planning to put a film on."[34] She paused before reflectively looking back at the common room window. "That is, Good Sister Robin will put a film on once she's figured out how to work the video player."[35]

"I want to help you free the duck," said Magda.

"I'm not sure that's anything to do with you," said Good Sister June. "And aren't you allergic to most animals?"

Magda shrugged. "I heard you all talking about it. I want to be there."

"You were listening?"

....

34 *Make Sure You're Crouching When It's Switched On: A Guide to Helicopter Maintenance.* It is quite a straightforward film but there are some scary bits.

35 Before DVDs, we had videos. They were big and rather bulky, but sometimes very useful on a rainy day.

"No," said Magda.[36]

Good Sister June shook her head. "You need to go back to the common room, Magda. It's raining. You should be inside. I shan't say it again."

A strange expression passed over Magda's face. It was a mixture of jealousy, anger, and something else that Good Sister June did not quite understand. "But it's not fair!" Magda said breathlessly. "Ever since Elizabeth got here, you've let her break the rules and I don't understand why."

"Nobody's broken any rules," said Good Sister June.[37]

"Elizabeth has done nothing *but* break rules," Magda said furiously. "She's helping Chrissie with her homework, and she's been allowed to keep a pet, and now she's allowed to wander around outside whenever she wants. How is that even remotely fair?"

Good Sister June had never really liked Magda DeWitt, and sometimes it was really very hard not to tell her of this fact. This is why Good Sister June said nothing.

It was not a terribly helpful decision.

Magda rolled her eyes. "I know about ducks too," she said, gesturing at *Mallardus Amazonica*, which was currently having a nap under a pile of straw and deeply unaware of all of the drama happening before it. "I'll know more than Elizabeth about them, you watch me, and someday I'll know more than all of you about—everything."

"Magda," said Good Sister June.

....

36 The lie didn't convince either of them.
37 Neither of them believed that lie, either.

"I'll never forget the way you've treated me," said Magda.

Good Sister June sighed and said, "I don't want to put you in detention, Magda, but you're leaving me no choice."

Magda gave her a steely look. "You'll regret this. Maybe not now, maybe not even next week, but there'll be a time—soon—when you'll be sorry. All of you!"

Good Sister June did one of the most heroic things that she had ever done at that point. She did not laugh.[38] "Off you go," she said. "Quickly, now. I imagine you'll already have missed the credits."

And Magda, at last, went.

---

38 Trust me, it was a close thing.

SAYING GOODBYE

Neither Chrissie nor Elizabeth looked surprised to see Good Sister June already in the yard, waiting for them. In truth the encounter with Magda had left the nun a little nervous about leaving the duck by itself. She was not sure what Magda could do, or indeed what she had intended to do, but the thought that Magda might do something had made Good Sister June find shelter in that little yard and wait there in silence until the other girls came.

And when they did arrive, Good Sister June looked at Elizabeth and saw the fine tension on her face and the pale edges of her skin. "How are you feeling?" she said, even though she suspected she already knew the answer. "Elizabeth, I know this is going to be difficult but we're both here to help you through it. You just tell us what you need."

Elizabeth looked at Good Sister June, and it was as if she'd never seen her before. She said, "This is a drake, but you can also call it a duck. It's both."

Good Sister June glanced at Chrissie in surprise, and Chrissie, who was sometimes very perceptive about this sort of thing, wrapped her arms around Elizabeth and squeezed her very tightly before letting her go.[39]

Elizabeth felt a little as if she might cry and because that might frighten the duck, she took a deep breath and counted to ten. When she reached nine, she felt her stomach start to settle and the lump in her throat disappear. "We should go now," she said. "I think it's going to start raining again."

But it didn't. The rain held off, and the four[40] of them walked out of the yard and down into the forest that surrounded the school. Winter could make the trees look like fingers and bone, but rain made them look like silver. And that evening, they shone.

They walked down the fine and lacy rabbit paths that led to the stream. Elizabeth was looking for the perfect place to let the duck go. The water had to be clear and quick flowing, and free of any plants or undergrowth that might impede the duck on its way. It had to be perfect. It had to be right.

When she found a good spot, she knelt down and let the duck slowly push itself into the running water. The duck moved forward just a little before stopping and twisting so that it was looking right back up at her. "You have come so far," whispered Elizabeth. "I'm so proud of you. Do you remember back when we first met? It was like you'd forgotten how to even be a duck. But I think you remember it now. I think you're ready

....

39 I must emphasize here that Chrissie did not hug both Elizabeth and the duck. She hugged Elizabeth, and let the duck stay at arm's length. She was a very nice girl but duck-hugging was not her forte.

40 Three humans, one duck.

to go home. You've got a long way to fly,[41] and you're going to make it all the way."

Chrissie and Good Sister June took a step back to give Elizabeth a moment of privacy. They both knew, as clearly as if they'd been told, that she wasn't just saying goodbye to the duck.

"I'll miss you," said Elizabeth. She pressed her face against the duck's feathers and closed her eyes. "Everyone always leaves me but I don't forget them. I thought I had, but I hadn't. You don't ever forget what people are. What they meant to you. And you made me remember that. Them. Everything. You made me want to remember. You made it not hurt." She eased her hands apart so that the duck's legs were free and she supported it until she felt its legs start to work in the water. A soft sound of excitement escaped its throat, and it gave her a last, quick look, before kicking purposefully forward. Within moments it was bobbing along the stream and then, before she had quite realized it, it had gone.

Elizabeth stood up and walked over to where Chrissie and Good Sister June were standing. They smiled when she got there, and pulled her in for a hug that said everything. The three of them stayed locked together for a long time before slowly peeling apart.

Good Sister June began to polish her glasses. "You might

---

41 She was not wrong. This small brown duck was a duck that did not live in the United Kingdom but rather several thousand miles away in the Amazon in a location that nobody knew about. Then.

see each other again. You never know." Her voice shook only a little. It was understandable, really.

Elizabeth smiled. "Maybe," she said, and as she looked at the two of them, she realized something. Chrissie and Good Sister June felt a little bit like family, and the feeling did not make her sad. If anything, it made something warm and solid burn inside her; something *good*.

"Thank you for everything," she said. "I'm ready to leave now. Let's go home."

And as the three of them walked back into school, they were so lost in the wonder of what had happened between them, they did not see Magda DeWitt curled up at the window of the North Tower bedroom.

Magda saw them, though.

In fact, she had seen the entire thing.

A BRIEF NOTE FROM YOUR NARRATOR

That is where we must leave Elizabeth, Magda, Chrissie, and Good Sister June for now, though I promise we will come back to them all soon. I need to jump many years ahead, to the day when Elizabeth gives birth to her daughter. Calla Rose North was born on one of the hottest days in one of the hottest Augusts ever recorded, and her father was not there to see it. He died just a few days before the birth of his daughter, thanks to an illness that had lain silently inside him for years and had only just decided to make itself known.

And when things like that happen, it is necessary to hold on to the good things in life.

Calla was Elizabeth's good thing. Elizabeth loved her daughter so fiercely that sometimes it made her scared. Calla was the reason Elizabeth kept going throughout those moments when the electricity bills stayed unpaid or when another job rejection came in the post. When Calla was a baby, Elizabeth wrapped her to her chest in a sling, and cleaned warehouses in the fine gray hours of the morning to earn some money, and only Calla's contented snores stopped her from giving up.

As you know, Elizabeth was very smart. She had left school

and gone to university, and learned more about ducks than you or I can ever imagine. In fact, by the time her daughter was born, Elizabeth knew more about ducks than anyone else alive.[42]

But knowing a lot about ducks wasn't any use in paying the bills.[43] Not in the slightest.

The money that her parents left her slid out of her fingers so quickly that some days she felt as if she'd never had it at all. So Elizabeth cleaned, and she saved, and she worked every job that she could, and somehow the two of them survived. Calla did her math homework by the light of a candle when the electricity was cut off, and Elizabeth figured out how to make a handful of carrots last for weeks when that was all that they had. When the television didn't work, they played games on scraps of paper, and when there was no paper, they imagined instead. It was not an easy childhood, nor was it an ideal one. Calla learned about food banks before she learned her own name, and yet, it did not matter because Elizabeth was with her throughout it all.

And as long as the two of them were together, nothing else mattered.

....

42 When you are very smart at something, you do not tend to think about the people who are almost as smart as you. And Magda DeWitt was one of those people. She had left school and gone to study and learn all about ducks, but she never managed to know as much as Elizabeth. This is the sort of thing that happens when you try to learn something that you do not wish to learn. Elizabeth loved learning and soaked up facts like a sponge. Magda did not love learning because she was angry, and jealous, and spent her days cursing the name of Elizabeth North every time she read about her.

Perhaps, upon reflection, it was best that Elizabeth did not think of her. But then, if she had, there would be no story to tell you.

43 Pun unintentional.

LIKE A COLD KALE SMOOTHIE WITH A SIDE ORDER OF BRUSSELS SPROUTS

Once, when she was very young, Calla had a particularly problematic day at school. First of all, she'd argued with Miranda Price, and then William Perry had stolen her paint before she'd finished with it, so she stole his lunch and then the two of them had ended up in detention which meant that she'd never finished her painting and she'd had to spend her afternoon in detention with a boy.[44]

But when her mum came to the school gates to pick her up, Calla realized that she had bigger problems to deal with. It was not the picking up that was the problem, because Elizabeth did this quite often when she remembered. The problem was the fact that she was wearing a laboratory coat with bright purple slippers and talking to a man in black who was, it seemed, trying to persuade her to get into the car with him.[45]

....

44 Some boys are quite pleasant, but William Perry was not one of those boys. He was, in fact, as pleasant as a cold kale smoothie with a side order of Brussels sprouts.

45 Now you and I both know that if somebody you don't know asks you to get into a car with them, then you run very quickly in the opposite direction. Elizabeth, however, was sometimes Not Great at remembering the important things in life.

Calla knew that her mum could sometimes be Not Very Good when it came down to practical things such as paying bills and how not to shrink socks in the washing machine, so she ran down the path to the gate and inserted herself between Elizabeth and the man and said, "Who are you?"

"He's very interested in ducks," Elizabeth said happily. "We were just talking about the aerodynamic qualities of the—"

"Nobody is interested in ducks," interrupted Calla. She knew that she was being rude, and she was not the sort of person to be rude by choice, but it had been a very bad day. She did not have either the time or the inclination to figure out how to be polite before she figured out who this man was and why he was talking to her mum.

Elizabeth looked appalled. "Calla."

Calla ignored her. "Who are you?" She rested her hands on her hips and glared at the man. He was not the sort of man you would typically see on an ordinary street. He was wearing a dark suit, with a symbol on the front pocket—it looked like a duck with its wings crossed behind its back, and the letters *M.O.* He did not look like social services, nor did he look like the police. He looked like something else, and Calla did not like that. Not one bit.

"Another time," said the man, which was the sort of reply that really did not answer the question. He nodded at Elizabeth, before getting back into the car and driving off in a rather hurried fashion.

"Mum, what were you doing?" said Calla. "You know you don't talk to strange people without me—"

It must be admitted at this point that Elizabeth had already

50

forgotten what the man had asked her. He had said something about ducks and then something about her going with him to help him out on a job, but she hadn't been paying much attention. She had been working out an elaborate cipher based on custard creams and jammie dodgers.[46]

"Calla, I talk to people every day," said Elizabeth. She decided to hold back on sharing her thoughts on biscuit-based codes with her daughter. "I've had a very busy afternoon."

Calla shook her head. "So busy you forgot to get dressed? Mum, we talked about this."

A sudden look of horror flashed across Elizabeth's face. She looked down at her clothes before visibly relaxing. "Honestly, I thought I hadn't put any clothes on at all for a moment there. Calla, don't frighten me like that." She grinned at her daughter. "Look, let's talk about my day instead. Much more fun. Did you know that the Qvada duck could actually form human language? Obviously there was a certain duckish quality to its speech, and the occasional extra quack in a sentence, but the written records still survive. I was reading them today, and it was terribly fond of discussing the weather. Can you imagine?"

It was not the best time for Elizabeth to babble. She only did this when she was very excited about something, or had a productive session in the archives. Either way, it was difficult

....

46 It must be noted that this was not the first time Elizabeth had been approached by strange people about her research. Usually she was too busy thinking of Victoria sponges and wingspans to pay them much attention. You, however, should pay very close attention indeed. (Aren't I helpful? Honestly, I am the best storyteller.)

enough to deal with on a good day, and a good day was the very opposite of what Calla had had.

But sometimes it took Elizabeth a long time to realize this.

"You're very quiet. Is it because of your detention? The school phoned me and told me you'd be late and well, I think you know that if you do the crime, Calla, then you have to do the time. Anyway. Enough of that sort of thing. Let's go back to my day. After I was done reading about the Qvada duck, I found a reference to *Mallardus Amazonica*—it's resistant to nearly every illness known to—"

Calla held up her hand. "Have you seen what you look like?"

"Yes," said Elizabeth. "But what about the duck—?"

"You're wearing a laboratory coat and slippers. Can't you just look normal? Can't you just—for once—try?"

"But I'm not normal," Elizabeth said blankly. "Nobody is. Everybody is extraordinary. We all burn with potential, and to seek for the normal in the world is to limit yourself. Why on earth would you ever want to do that?"

"Normal deals with envelopes," said Calla.

The pile of angry envelopes on the corner of their dining room table had been growing and they'd had lentils for tea for the past four nights in a row. Calla knew the signs that money was tight. She had known the signs all her life.

And realizing that her daughter knew all of this suddenly made Elizabeth very sad. "You shouldn't have to deal with this sort of thing," she said. "I'm so sorry."

"But I do have to deal with it," said Calla. And as always when she and her mother fought, her words began to go somewhere that she did not expect. "Can't you get a proper job somewhere, or can't you teach or work in an office or, I don't know, do something that doesn't involve you coming to school and looking like this and *talking—about—ducks*."

Elizabeth smiled. She had wanted to cry moments earlier, but now, wonderfully, she could do nothing but smile.

Calla said, "Stop it."

But, if anything, Elizabeth's smile grew a little bit wider. She said, "Oh, Calla, I think you're ready. I honestly do."

"For what?" Calla was still annoyed and bubbling over with feelings that she did not quite understand, but she was also interested in the way that her mother was looking at her. She knew a lot of the expressions her mother wore, but this one was brand-new.

"This," said Elizabeth. "I want you to take what I'm about to say very seriously because I think it might be the most important thing I ever tell you."

"More important than the speech habits of the Qvada duck?"

Elizabeth nodded. "Yes," she said.

LIFE LESSONS COURTESY OF LINDA AND FREDERICK

Calla reached out and took her mum's hand. The two of them walked over to a nearby bench that looked out over the park. There was a small dedication on the back of the bench that read *For Linda and Frederick,*[47] *who loved this view and each other.* Calla sat on *Frederick* and her mum sat on *Linda.*

"I know I'm not the most straightforward person in the world," said Elizabeth. "And I know that sometimes our life isn't as simple as it could have been. There have been moments when I've thought that I'm doing it wrong. So many moments when I've wondered if I've done the right thing, made the right choices . . ."

"I can't imagine you not making the right choices," said Calla simply.

Elizabeth smiled. She was trying very hard not to cry, and that sort of comment did not make it any easier. "I've made a lot of mistakes," she said. "Ever since your father died, it's

....

47 Linda Bowles and Frederick Parsons met in 1954, while walking their dogs. Linda had a golden retriever called Susan, and Frederick had a small terrier called Darcy, and it was love at first sight for both dogs and humans.

just been the two of us and all I've done is try to get from one day to the next. I'm not real-world smart, Calla. I can't rewire a plug or fix the boiler. If I could, then things would be different, but I can't. I just know a lot about ducks. And I could have made a lot of money from that, don't get me wrong, but the way—it wasn't right. Ethics are a costly business, and mine cost me . . . well, a lot."

Calla stared at her mother. She'd never known any of this.

"Sometimes I wonder if I made the right call," Elizabeth said dreamily. "We would have been rich, and I'd have been able to give you everything. And that's all I've ever wanted to do, but I couldn't do it in the way that they wanted. *Mallardus Amazonica* is special. Some people want to use it for the wrong reasons. I'm just trying to keep it safe."

Calla squeezed her mum's hand. It was the sort of squeeze that said everything she could not even begin to figure out the words for.

Elizabeth gave her a teary smile. "I need to make a difference. I still do. One day that little brown bird is going to change our lives. I know it. I won't stop fighting for that until it happens. And neither should you."

Calla shook her head. "I just hate it. I'm sick of everything."

"No you're not," said Elizabeth. "That's not you. Look, tell me something. If I could grant you one wish right now, what would it be?"

"To not go to school," said Calla, and a look of surprise flashed across her face. She very suddenly realized that she hadn't been upset about what her mum was wearing. Or her talking about ducks. It was school. It had been about the way going to school made her feel all along. "I just want to grow up and be the person who decides what I get to do instead of being told all the time. I'm sick of people bossing me around. You don't get away with anything when you're a kid, and it's not fair. All I have done today is be yelled at and everything's gone wrong and I hate it, I hate it."

Elizabeth looked at her. "You are miraculous."

"I don't feel it," said Calla.

"Then you must be brave and make yourself feel it," said Elizabeth. She wrapped her arms around Calla and pulled her in tight. Calla closed her eyes and squeezed her right back, as hard as she could. It was definitely a Squeeze Each Other as Tightly as Possible sort of moment.

When they were done, Elizabeth took a few moments to gather herself. "My mum told me how to be brave a long time ago. Whenever I've been very, very sad and very, very scared, and I have been both more than you know, I have always tried to remember what she said. And that was to remember who I am and to never let that go." Her voice shook, just a tiny bit. "I never want you to be sad or scared, but I know that life will bring it to you sooner or later. I just hope that when that moment comes, even if you can't remember anything else, you'll remember how to be *you*."

Calla opened her eyes and looked up at her mother. She pulled up the collar of her coat and used it to wipe the tears off her face. She said, "I'm sorry," and even though she wasn't quite sure what she was apologizing for, she knew that she had to say it.

"It's all right." Elizabeth rummaged in her lab coat pocket

and produced two chocolate wafers. "Oh, look," she said, trying to appear innocent but failing quite substantially. "I accidentally-on-purpose brought us both chocolate biscuits to eat on the way home. Do you mind if we stay and eat them here instead?"

"No," said Calla with a small smile. "No, I do not."

BUT THEN EVERYTHING CHANGED

Of course it did, for this is a story, and stories thrive on conflict.

And Calla's conflict was a most unexpected thing.

It was a cream envelope that arrived very quietly one morning.

THE WAY IT ALL BEGAN

Elizabeth and Calla had had problems before in their family. They were especially used to the sorts of problems that came in important-looking envelopes and had things like FINAL DEMAND and PAY NOW written in red on the outside of them because they were the sorts of problems that required Calla and her mother to shop from the bottom shelf in the supermarket,[48] pay for that food with pennies, and turn off all of the lights in the house, before being solved. But they could be solved, that was the thing. They were solved, and after they were solved, they would have a slice of cake and all would be well in the North household.

Nothing about that little cream envelope that came in the post that morning seemed like it might be the sort of thing to turn everything upside down.[49] Calla saw it first.

....

48 You might not know about shopping from the bottom shelf, and you are lucky if you do not, but the bottom shelf is where the cheapest food is. The tins that are more juice than fruit, more sauce than spaghetti hoops. They are shelved so low because the supermarket wants you to buy the more expensive things, but sometimes you simply cannot do that.

49 Spoiler (I am becoming increasingly comfortable with this expression! Thank you, Good Sister Gwendolyn!): It does.

She picked it up from the doormat and left it on her mother's desk before heading off to school as normal. She had lunch and double math and argued with Miranda Price as normal. But when she came home and found her mother sitting downstairs with the table set for dinner, Calla realized that there was something happening in their house that was very not-normal indeed.

"Hi," said Calla. She placed her bag down on the floor and studied her mother's face carefully. "What's going on?"

"What makes you think that there's something going on?" said Elizabeth.

Calla counted off the reasons inside her head: Elizabeth was out of her study, and that never happened until it was dark or *Coronation Street*[50] had started; and the table was set for dinner, but they never ate at the table. Calla used a corner of it for her homework and for the past five years, Elizabeth had used the rest of it to store a life-size model of a duck's digestive system. She'd made the model for a lecture, back when she'd taught at the university, and the model had lived there ever since. Until today. The gizzards, esophagus, and proventriculus had now been replaced by place mats. Calla hadn't even known that they owned place mats.

All of this meant that her mother was trying to tell her that something unusual had happened and that she didn't know where to begin.

....

50 We all have our weaknesses.

"A lot of reasons," Calla said eventually. "But mainly because I think that you've been in the kitchen."

She could smell something cooking, and it was definitely not the burning sort of cooking that was Elizabeth's specialty.

"Somebody's offered me a job," said Elizabeth.

BELINDA FREEMAN

"But who?" said Calla. It had been a long time since she'd heard the J-word in their house. She couldn't think who would have offered her mum an actual, real-life job.

"Do you know who Belinda Freeman is?" said Elizabeth. Her eyes were bright and excited, and she didn't wait for Calla to reply. "She is possibly the most important duck researcher in the entire world. I mean, she is basically the absolute queen of ducks. Apart from me."

"What's the job, though?" said Calla, who didn't actually care about Belinda Freeman in the slightest.

Elizabeth gestured at the cream envelope. "Read it," she said. Calla picked up the envelope and slid out a letter that had been written on paper so thick it almost resembled cardstock. Nobody sent handwritten letters anymore, and definitely not handwritten letters that looked like this. Every word looked like a piece of art.

"It's very curly," she said carefully, as she tried to figure out what the first word said. "She should have emailed. It would have been easier to read."

"She's very old," said Elizabeth. "If I'm honest, I thought she'd retired. Nobody's seen her for years. Somebody must have made her a very good offer to come back to work. Anyhow, do you want me to read the letter?" Calla nodded and handed it back.

Elizabeth held it in front of her and cleared her throat.

"Dear Elizabeth. My name is Belinda Freeman and I would like to offer you a job. I have been offered funding for a research trip to the Amazon to study the breeding grounds of the rare Mallardus Amazonica. *I would rather like you to be part of this endeavor. The trip would be purely for conservation purposes. Our backers are covering all expenses, and they're also offering a very generous daily stipend[51] of—"*

Elizabeth paused and then said the number very carefully, and Calla stared at her.

"That's a lot of zeros," she said. "I don't even know what that number is."

Elizabeth nodded. "I didn't either," she said. "I had to work it out on my fingers and toes and then I had to borrow some extra fingers before I finally worked it out. It's a lot."

The two of them paused in respectful silence of this, before Elizabeth gathered herself and read the rest of the letter.

"We will be leaving in only a few weeks and shall spend the next six months in the Amazon. I appreciate this is

---

51 This is a fancy word for pocket money. For some reason I've yet to figure out, adults get a bit upset if you call it "pocket money."

*a lot to ask of you, Elizabeth, especially on such short
notice, but your knowledge would be invaluable to us.*
Mallardus Amazonica *is such an elusive beast, and
you're the only person in the world who knows where
it may be."*[52]

"Is that true?" said Calla. "Do you really know where it is?"

Elizabeth nodded. "It's true," she said. "Well, sort of. I know
where it *might* be. There have been people who've wanted me
to tell them, but I never have because I've tried to keep it safe.
But this is a lot of money, Calla. It might help me to protect
Mallardus Amazonica, and use my knowledge of it for good.
I've wanted to take this trip my whole life, but it's so expensive
and I've never had the money. But let me finish reading her
letter.

*"I hope that this offer is tempting enough for you to
consider. Please get back to me forthwith with your
decision. Yours in knowledge, Belinda."*

Calla took a deep breath. "What does *forthwith* mean?" she
said.

"As soon as possible."

"You're going to go."

Elizabeth nodded again, but slower this time. "We're strug-
gling. More than you know." She gestured at the pile of enve-

---

52 Pay attention to this point. It's kind of extremely important for everything
that follows.

lopes in the corner of the room. They were always high, but they usually went down. They hadn't gone down for a very long while. Some of them were even beginning to gather dust.

"But what about your articles?" said Calla. "Or the cleaning jobs—"

"Nobody's buying anything, and the temp agency's had no shifts for me since March. I've been keeping us going with my savings for a long time, Calla, but they weren't even enough to begin with. It's starting to run out."

Calla held herself very still. "I don't know what that means for us," she said. Thoughts began spinning through her head. Thoughts of the people who'd taken their TV that one Christmas. The people who'd cut off their electricity. The people who'd tried to split them up. She was very certain that she couldn't deal with that happening all over again.

"I don't know what it means, either," said Elizabeth. "But I do know that if I go on this trip then we've got a chance. We'll be able to pay our bills for the next two years, and that's two years we don't have right now. If I rent the house out while I'm away, we can get a tenant in and that will help us even more. We'll be able to put some money away for a rainy day. It's kind of the answer to our prayers." Elizabeth had to stop speaking then because she wasn't able to say anything else. It was all too much.

Calla started to feel a bit strange inside her tummy. There was something that her mother was forgetting and Calla rather thought that the something might be her. Elizabeth was talking like this was a trip for one person. Not two. "But what's going to happen to me?"

"Oh! I forgot."

"You—forgot me?" This wasn't making things any better. Calla was used to her mum being forgetful, but it was always about other things. Not her.

"That's not what I meant," said Elizabeth. "I couldn't ever forget about you. You're the first thing I think of in the morning and the last at night. When I read Belinda's letter, I knew I needed to make this work in a way that suited us all, and that involves you going to school. Not the one you're at now, but the one I went to when I was younger. I phoned them, and they've got space for you and you can even stay there over Christmas with the other boarders and it's all sorted out. There's really nothing to be concerned about in the slightest. Isn't that wonderful?"

Calla did not think it was wonderful. She felt rather as if she wanted to cry, and one of the things that Calla North knew about crying was that if you wanted to do it, then you really should. So she simply shook her head, and ran upstairs, and then she cried.

MALLARDUS AMAZONICA

Elizabeth took a deep breath. She knew that she should go and talk to Calla about what had just happened, but she also knew that her daughter needed a few moments by herself. And so, instead, she thought about a small brown duck that she'd released back into the wild all those years ago and how that little brown duck might now be the solution to all their problems.

After a long while, Elizabeth stood up. She went into the kitchen, turned the oven off, and left the casserole inside to stay warm. She picked up the biscuit tin and walked upstairs and sat down on the top step, just outside of Calla's bedroom door. She picked out a chocolate wafer, and the last white chocolate finger, and waited.

After a few minutes, Calla came out of her room and sat down next to her. The two of them squeezed together on the top stair, and Elizabeth offered Calla the last white chocolate finger. It was both the best biscuit[53] and a peace offering. Sometimes Elizabeth could be very wise that way.

....

53 Though I admit a pink wafer is a similarly wonderful thing.

When the two of them had finished their biscuits, Elizabeth put the tin down and said, "I'm sorry." She rubbed her hand on Calla's back. "I didn't tell you properly. I was overexcited and I didn't think about your feelings. Will you accept my apology?"

Calla nodded. "Yes," she said slowly. "But it's a bit—I mean—what if you don't come back? The Amazon is a long way away." Her voice felt very shaky, and her head hurt. The bit after crying was always the worst bit, but sitting like this with her mother was perfect. It felt like it was just the two of them against the world and that was something Calla understood very well.

Elizabeth smiled in that pale, watery way that people do when everything is a little bit tender inside of them. "I'll phone you. Every minute that I can. I'll check in on the way there—we'll make it so that you know when to expect me—and then I'll call you when we set up base camp, and that'll all be in the first week—"

"You don't even properly know where you're going."

"If you're going to worry about me, then I won't go."

"You have to go," said Calla. She swatted Elizabeth's arm lightly and tried to ignore the wobble in her throat. "You've wanted this your whole life. The ducks need you. And we need the money."

Elizabeth shook her head. "You need me more."

Calla bit her lip. She thought of those times when the pile of IMPORTANT and FINAL NOTICE envelopes had grown almost as tall as her head, and that Christmas when they'd not been able to afford the heating, and the look on her mum's face when she'd read out Belinda Freeman's letter.

"I'll be all right," Calla said.[54] "It's just going to be six months."

"Would it help if I told you a bit more about the school?" said Elizabeth. She picked out another biscuit for each of them. "It was a good place. We did our work and the nuns, I think, just marked it and threw it in a cupboard or something. Nobody really cared about that sort of thing. Now that I think about it, I bet all of our old schoolbooks are still there.[55] The nuns weren't for doing dull things like tidying up. They were more for making chocolate chip cookies and sharing recipe tips. Good Sister Honey could make a mean Baked Alaska, let me tell you. Don't ever underestimate a nun. They are remarkable women. Good Sister June was my favorite[56] apart from Chrissie. I mean, technically she wasn't a nun then, but she is now."

"Who's Chrissie?" said Calla.

"My best friend," said Elizabeth. "We lost touch after school. She went to teacher training college and then she decided to become a nun and teach at the school. One of the rules is that the staff don't have any personal belongings. I couldn't call or text Chrissie without it going through the landline, and then when our phone got cut off and things happened, I had other things to think about."

Calla knew all about other things to think about. She had

....

54 And if ever a sentence was the very definition of bravery, then this one was.
55 They were. This is an important point that you should remember. The nuns were very good at being nuns, but they were not the best at throwing things away. Luckily enough.
56 Whilst this is a very nice thing for Elizabeth to say, I feel it necessary to point out that she had not met many people at that point in her life.

spent her life thinking about other things. "But I need a phone," she said, "so you can call me. You have to call me."

"I won't forget."

Calla gave her mum a Look.

"I promise," said Elizabeth. "I've already arranged it so that you can take a phone to the school. It's all sorted. I'm buying you one and Good Sister June knows all about it. She understands that I need to phone you directly. I won't forget. I'll set reminders and—"

"All right," said Calla. "I'll do it. I'll go to the school."

"Are you—are you sure?" said Elizabeth.

Calla nodded. "Yes," she said, "but you have to bring me back a duck."

"I shall bring you *Mallardus Amazonica*," said Elizabeth. "It is the best duck."

"I don't really want a duck," said Calla.

"I know," said Elizabeth.

THE UNEXPECTED STRENGTH OF CALLA AND ELIZABETH NORTH

Once the decision was made, everything started to move very rapidly. The Good Sisters sent a list of essential requirements, and Calla and Elizabeth spent a whole two days shopping for everything that they needed. Calla had to have all her clothing labeled and then they had to find a brown trunk to pack all of her belongings in. Neither of them was quite sure what that meant until Elizabeth googled and found a picture from a website about schooling in Victorian times. She looked concerned. "I'm not sure if we can afford this. They look very expensive."

"Did you have a trunk when you were there?" asked Calla. She had finished balling up her black socks (knee high, six pairs)[57] and was officially Between Jobs.

"No. But to be fair, I don't think I would have noticed if I had two heads and three legs. It wasn't the easiest time in my life." Elizabeth tapped her fingers against her thigh and thought deeply for a moment. "I'm going to send an email to some of

---

[57] One on, one in the wash, and four in the cupboard for sock-based emergencies. You will be surprised at how often such things can occur.

my old friends at the university, and see if they've got something like this tucked away. It's the sort of weird thing they might have."

"I don't know why I can't have a rucksack like a normal person."

"Me neither," said Elizabeth. "I'm sorry. We should have finished this already. I made soup for supper[58] and everything."

"It won't burn," said Calla. She had, of course, already checked this.

"I don't know what I'm going to do without you," said Elizabeth. "Are you sure you're going to be all right without me? You just have to say the word and I'll cancel."

A part of Elizabeth really wanted Calla to tell her that she didn't have to go.

A part of Calla really wanted to tell Elizabeth that she didn't have to go.

"You have to go," Calla said firmly.[59]

"I might die of hunger without you to help me," said Elizabeth.

"They *do* have food in the Amazon," said Calla. "Probably even cake shops, too. The expedition should have supplies, but you should probably buy something extra. Just put it in the plane. Make sure it can still take off, though."

"Did you know that *Mallardus Amazonica* can lift twice its own body weight?" Elizabeth said dreamily. "It's a rather

---

58 She had indeed made soup. It was tomato and came out of a can that had been on sale. It was the sort of recipe that Calla approved of very much because her mother could not mess it up.

59 And, I think, a little bit bravely.

marvelous bird. It's very small, very brown, but with a distinctively long bill."

Calla gave Elizabeth a Look.

Elizabeth grinned back at her before twisting to tap out a swift email on her laptop. "Fingers crossed this gets you a trunk, or we'll just have to get you a case from the charity shop and hope for the best." She pressed SEND. "It's a good thing your last day at school is tomorrow; otherwise we wouldn't have time to do everything before you go."

Calla wondered whether she should give her mum another Look but decided against it. Sometimes Elizabeth could be very clever but sometimes she could not, and thinking that Calla's last day at school was a Good Thing was one of the moments when she was being Not. It was because of this that Calla decided to change the subject. "Tell me more about the Good Sisters," she said.

Elizabeth looked thoughtful. "They helped me out a lot when your grandparents died," she said. "They really helped me learn who I was. My mum had named them as my guardians in case something happened. And well, when something did happen, Good Sister June stepped in. She was my guardian until I was eighteen."

"Do I have a guardian?"

"Two," said Elizabeth. "Good Sister June and Mrs. Merryweather from downstairs."[60]

....

60 You may be wondering why Calla was not sent to stay with Mrs. Merryweather. It had been a possibility Elizabeth considered before remembering that Mrs. Merryweather was a delightful soul but had once confused ducks with geese and so was Not Really Suitable When You Come to Think About It.

"But why did you pick Mrs. Merryweather?"

"She makes an excellent Victoria sponge," said Elizabeth. "Now, will you please hand me that sweater?"

A SUNNY DAY IN MARCH

Calla's last day at school was full of sunshine. It also involved cake, and presents, and a long and complicated fight with Miranda Price. The fight began when Miranda Price said, "Is it true you have no money?" and when Calla got to lunch, Miranda Price said, "Is it true that you've never bought any clothes that weren't secondhand?" and when Calla got to afternoon registration, Miranda Price said, "Why is your mum so weird?" and it was then that Calla told her to shut up, which was, to be frank, quite the act of restraint.

"Shut up," said Calla.

"Whatever," said Miranda Price. "I'll make a new friend."

And that was when Calla realized that Miranda Price had never been her friend in the slightest.

Calla didn't talk to anybody for the rest of the day, and when the bell rang she was the first to grab her bag and run out. She went home via the chip shop instead of going the normal way and counted out the last of her long-saved pennies for a cone of chips. She put extra salt and extra vinegar on them, and walked down to the pier where she ate them in front of the setting sun. The sky turned pink and rose and gold, and as

Calla ate the best chips she'd ever had in her life, she slowly started to realize that she wasn't going back to that school. No more fights with Miranda Price. No more detentions because of William Perry. Not for six months at least, and maybe not ever again.[61]

When Calla got home, she realized that her mum had been cooking. She couldn't smell anything burning, but Elizabeth was standing in the kitchen looking hopeful, and the table was already set, which indicated either dinner or the offer of a trip to the Amazon. As she could rule out the latter, Calla knew that dinner was imminent. She put her bag down in the corner of the room and began to pull her shoes off. "What's for tea?"

"It's rather remarkable how flexible language is," began Elizabeth. "Did you know that the word *duck* is derived from Germanic origins? Essentially it's a *diving bird*, which is ironic if we consider *Mallardus*—"

"I had a fight with Miranda Price."

"I'm sure it was justified," said Elizabeth.[62] "I've found tenants for the house. They're a young couple with a baby and one of them is a scientist, which is terribly exciting. We had quite the wonderful chat. Her husband is an artist, and I've given him permission to do whatever he likes inside the house as long as he makes it good on our return. Also his favorite film is *Howard the Duck* and I think that's a good sign even though it's a film that's absolutely full of biological inaccuracies."

....

61 Happiness. Endless, sudden, incomprehensible happiness.
62 Who had met Miranda Price.

Calla decided to focus on the important things. "What are we having for tea?" she asked again. The casserole the other day had been surprisingly good, even though due to Circumstances and Having Biscuits on the Stairs they'd ended up having it three hours later than teatime should have been.

"It was meant to be roast chicken and salad," said Elizabeth.

"And what is it now?" said Calla.

"Salad," said Elizabeth.

GOODBYE, CHARLIE NORTH

One day to buy last-minute things, another day to pack everything that they'd forgotten, and then all of a sudden, like a trip to the dentist or an exam that you'd forgotten all about, it was here. The last day. The worst day.

Calla and her mum went by the graveyard on their way to the station and while Elizabeth sat on a bench[63] and tried to hide her tears, Calla sat on the grass and told her dad everything. She explained about the expedition, and leaving one school and going to another, and how Elizabeth had to go abroad to make sure they could pay their bills and maybe shop from the top shelf in the supermarket every now and then. Once she had covered all of that, Calla reached the most difficult point of the conversation.

And so, as you should always do when you reach a difficult part of a conversation, Calla stopped speaking and took a moment to make sure that she had all her words in the right

---

63 *For Leon and Elsie; in memory of all the times that they played cards with the grandchildren and stole all of their pocket money.*

order. She placed her hand palm-flat on the grass and studied the headstone[64] in front of her.

"I'll never forget you," said Calla when she felt that she was able to speak. "Neither of us will, I promise, but we have to do this and that means you're going to be alone for a while. Mum will be somewhere in the Amazon, and I'm going to school, and you're going to have to be brave. But after it's all done, I'll find her and she'll find me, and then we'll come back and be together." She thought that she might want to cry when she said that, and so when she finished speaking, she held her breath and waited for it to happen. But it didn't. She just felt a strange sense of calm. They had been coming to the graveyard all her life, and giving her dad the news was part of her life. He might have died just before she was born, but that didn't mean that he was a stranger.

"You like chocolate but not hot chocolate," said Calla. "You would eat so much jelly and ice cream that you couldn't move without moaning. Your surname was so long and silly that instead of asking Mum to take yours when you got married, you took hers. And you are the bravest one of us all and I will tell you everything when I get back. Every single last bit."

When Elizabeth came over, Calla pretended not to notice that her mum had been crying. They didn't have any biscuits on hand, so this was probably the best thing to do under the circumstances. She did squeeze Elizabeth's hand just a little bit, so that she knew that she had noticed her crying but

---

64 *Charlie North, beloved always.*

wasn't mentioning it, and Elizabeth squeezed Calla's hand right back to say thank you.

"Have you updated him with all the news?"

Calla nodded. A part of her wanted to stay here forever but she knew that that wasn't possible. But even though she knew it, that didn't make her stop wanting it. It was the sort of wanting that came with eating too much ice cream. You want to stay in the moment almost more than anything, even though you know that it won't work out well in the end.

"Okay, then," said Elizabeth. "We have to go now."

"All right," said Calla. "I'm ready."

THE 11:33 TRAIN TO LITTLE HAMPDEN

Because they had spent so long saying goodbye to her dad, a thing that neither Elizabeth nor Calla was remotely sorry for, they arrived at the station at eleven twenty. This left them with just thirteen minutes to buy Calla some sweets for the trip, to get her to the right platform, and to say goodbye. They pushed through the station and as they reached the shop, Elizabeth ran in and came out almost instantly with a bar of milk chocolate and honeycomb. It was Calla's favorite and the gesture almost made her cry. She distracted herself from doing so by checking that her mum had actually paid for it.[65] "I paid at the self-service till," Elizabeth said proudly. "Didn't have to queue. Now, which platform do we need?"

They arrived on platform five with two minutes to spare and by the time they'd figured out where their carriage was going to stop, there was only a minute to go and the shape of the train was already on the horizon. All that was left for Calla and

---

65 As I am sure you know by now, sometimes Elizabeth forgot how to deal with the real world if it didn't quack.

Elizabeth was a goodbye but, as everybody knows, a goodbye is not a thing to be rushed.

And neither of them knew where to begin with theirs.

"Did you know that the Gunnison duck returns to the nest where it was born?" said Elizabeth as the train to Little Hampden pulled up. Her voice was rather faint, and her grip on Calla's shoulder was rather tight. "Every year, wherever it might be in the world, it flies back to where it was born. The pull of home is so strong. It always comes back to the nest."

A group of football fans pushed their way off the train, shouting and cheering, but for Calla the station was practically deserted. All that mattered was her mum. She let go of her suitcase and flung herself at Elizabeth, wrapping her arms around her waist and hugging her so tightly that it suddenly felt as though she might never let go.

"I like the Gunnison duck," said Calla, when she eventually released Elizabeth. "It's my absolute favorite."

The two of them looked at each other for a second longer before Calla gritted her teeth and clambered up onto the train. Elizabeth threw the suitcase up to her. They hadn't had time to find a trunk. Neither of them cared. Their eyes met. The door closed. Neither of them moved until the other was out of sight, and even then Calla stayed by the train door and Elizabeth stayed on the now-deserted platform until the station cleaners came along and asked her to move.

ENCOUNTERING THE LOCAL PENGUINS

After three hours and thirteen minutes, the train slid quietly into Little Hampden station and stopped. It was the final station on the line, and so there was no rush. Calla knew she couldn't miss her stop. Her mother had told her this in a comforting sort of way, despite both of them knowing it was not comforting in the slightest, and so Calla took the time to have a little cry before she got up and grabbed her suitcase off the luggage rack.

By the time she reached the platform, it was deserted. Calla didn't let herself think about that. Instead, she thought about her mum and how she'd be on her way to the airport right now. They'd looked up the trains together, and checked out the times. Calla had even written them all down and highlighted when Elizabeth would need to change trains to get her connection. After that, they'd planned out when Elizabeth needed to make her first phone call to Calla, and decided that the first would be when she landed in South America.[66] Two plane rides,

----

66 The second would be when she hit base camp, and the third at a point to be arranged after that. These are important things for you to know, trust me.

two days. They had thought about having the first when she got to the airport but it would have been too soon. Goodbyes were not the sorts of wounds to be opened easily.

"Hello," said a voice behind Calla.

Calla let out a tiny scream.

"That's not the reaction that I was after," said the voice. It turned out to belong to a tall woman dressed all in black, with a white scarf wrapped around her head.

"Who are you?" said Calla.

The woman grinned. "Very good. You should always check who somebody is. My name's Good Sister Christine. I am, as you might have gathered, a nun. I'm here to pick up a girl called Calla North who's going to be with us for six months whilst her mum goes off on an expedition to the Amazon. I was going to be here to meet Calla from the train, were it not for the fact that the car didn't start and Good Sister Gwendolyn had mislaid her wrench."

Calla stared at the nun in wonder. She sounded exactly like her mum. It was both comforting and slightly terrifying.

Good Sister Christine clapped her hands together. "I don't need to be Agatha Christie to work out that you are my new pupil in question and that providence has looked kindly upon my poor time-management skills."

"Who's Agatha Christie?" said Calla.

"A writer," said Good Sister Christine. "She once wrote that . it was worth dying to eat cake.[67] A particular cake. Not any

....

67 I must disagree with dear Agatha because it is not worth dying to eat any-
     thing. If you're dead, how will you know you've enjoyed it?

84

cake. A rather ridiculous sentiment, if you ask me. Totally disregards the appeal of pastries. A well-timed savory can be much more powerful than a cupcake.[68] But we can talk more about this sort of thing in the car. Come along."

And so Calla did.

---

68 I am very fond of Good Sister Christine, but she is Quite Wrong here.

GOOD SISTER CHRISTINE

The car was small and blue and very round. It looked like the sort of thing that very little children drew and told you it was a "car" when in fact, it looked more like an alien. The headlights even looked a little bit like eyes. Good Sister Christine opened the back door, took the suitcase, and swung it onto the back seat. There really wasn't that much room to begin with. Half of the back seat was already full of dusty piles of books. Calla could still see the marks of fingerprints where they'd been picked up. "Where do you want me to sit?" she asked, trying to figure it all out.

"On the hood. Just make sure you hold on as I go around the corners." Good Sister Christine caught sight of the look on Calla's face. "I'm joking. You shall sit in the front with me and I'll tell you everything about the school and answer all your concerns in a very supportive manner. You really do look rather terrified and there's no need to be. It's a good school. I should know, I went here myself when I was young. I was friends with your mum, as a matter of fact."

"You're Chrissie," said Calla, suddenly putting two and two together. She stared at the nun as she got in the car. "Aren't you?"

Good Sister Christine nodded. "I am," she said. "I was best friends with your mum until we just lost touch. You know how it is."

Calla did not know how *it* was but she had the sneaking suspicion that this was the sort of thing adults said when they didn't want to admit that they Weren't Actually Very Good at Adulting. She also had the sneaking suspicion that Good Sister Christine might not appreciate this being pointed out to her, so she did not say anything. Adults, in Calla's experience, were very complicated creatures.[69]

Good Sister Christine turned the engine on and started to reverse carefully out of the car park.[70] "You'll have a good time here. I promise you will. But if you need anything, then you come to me. I'll try and do my best by you." This little speech took them to the end of the lane and as Good Sister Christine waited at the junction for nonexistent traffic, she gave Calla a quick look. "You really are very quiet. Is everything all right?"

No, thought Calla. "Yes," she said.

"You don't have to be nervous," said Good Sister Christine. The little car lurched forward in a manner that said quite the opposite. "There's nothing to worry about."

Calla gave her a Look. She had not expected to be giving Looks this early in her new life, but Good Sister Christine

----

69 She is not wrong.

70 There was really no need for her to be careful because the nearest car was, at that point, fifteen miles away. It belonged to Mr. Harold Richardson, the local police officer and firefighter (Little Hampden is a small village and one man does everything), who was at that moment visiting his brand-new granddaughter in town.

really did remind her a lot of Elizabeth. "My mum's on her way to the Amazon and last week she forgot how to lace up her shoes."

"She was always distracted when she was excited. I bet this trip has her mind completely blown. She's brilliant, Calla, you know that, and I'm sure you also know that she's been planning this trip for years. She was planning it when I knew her. She'd make notes in her prep book about the rainforest, and she handed in assignments about ducks at every opportunity she got. I'll try to find her old notebooks if you like. We never throw anything away. It's a blessing and a curse."

"I've never seen anything she did as a kid," said Calla slowly. Elizabeth had long since sold everything in the house that could be sold, and much of those things had dated from her childhood. Sometimes Calla wondered if her mum had even had a childhood.

"I'll try to find you something in the store," said Good Sister Christine. "I'll bet when you read her old notes, you'll feel like she's standing right next to you. I suspect you're cut from a very similar cloth."

"I don't know what that means."

"You'll figure it out," said Good Sister Christine.

IN WHICH CALLA NORTH FORMS
A FIRST IMPRESSION

They drove out of the village and up a long and narrow road that seemed to get narrower and then narrower still until it was barely wider than the car itself. It was so tight that at points Calla felt as if she could lean out of the window and pick flowers from the hedges that they were driving past. Every now and then she couldn't stop herself from breathing in when a branch or a twig seemed to stretch out right across where she was sitting, but somehow the little car kept going.

"You really do look like Elizabeth," said Good Sister Christine, after one particularly close encounter with the side of the road. "I've followed her career in the news. We all have. We get the newspapers or use one of the computers in the library to find out what she was up to. We're so proud of what she's achieved."

Calla thought about the days when they could barely achieve light bulbs at their house and narrowed her eyes at Good Sister Christine. She was not sure that the nun quite understood how the world treated somebody who was very clever about ducks and having the right biscuit in the tin for emergencies but not clever enough about things like Paying Bills and Having

Enough Money for a Rainy Day. But she did not tell Good Sister Christine any of this, knowing that sometimes it is easier to let adults think what they want to think even if it is very far from the truth.[71] "I'm very proud as well," said Calla, which was, perhaps, the easiest thing to say under the circumstances.

"Does she still play around with codes?" asked Good Sister Christine. "I remember her doing that a lot. I was never sure why, though."

"The other day she renamed everything in the kitchen after cake."

"What?"

Calla sighed. She was so used to the strangeness of her life, sometimes she forgot others weren't. "She was sick of calling the fridge 'the fridge' so decided to call it Battenberg instead."

"But that's ridiculous," said Good Sister Christine. "It's clearly more of a lemon drizzle."

She stopped speaking as she wrenched the car around another corner and at last the School of the Good Sisters came into view.

The school is an important building in this story, so you will allow me the indulgence of describing it with some detail.

Much of the school was built by people with more ambition than sense. Rooms do not quite match up to windows and walls

---

71 It is an odd thing to realize but when you are little, you tend to look at adults as these magical beings who Know What to Do in Emergencies. The life that Calla had lived had told her the precise opposite: She knew that adults were simply trying to make it through the world. So she knew to let them pretend that they knew what they were doing, and to simply continue doing what she was going to do.

seem to be built in the middle of nowhere connecting nothing to nothing. The roofs are flat and leak during the lightest spell of rain. Unfortunately you can never quite predict from where or when the next leak will come and so there are certain corridors in the school that are, if I am honest, more bucket than carpet. Towers had been added in a haphazard sort of manner, most of which now house the girls' bedrooms.

The school was built from red brick, and almost all of it is encircled by a tall iron fence that is the sort of thing you might imagine being used in a Victorian zoo. It is not the most attractive of buildings and I fear, if you met it in the dark, you might want to run in the opposite direction. For example, as Calla North studied it, she realized that the front door looked more like a shadow than a door and that the windows on the upper floors were almost completely covered by ivy. The thought of sleeping in one of those rooms made a small shiver run up her spine and the only thing that stopped her from saying something was the fact that her mum had done it. And if she had, then so would Calla. She would be brave.

Whatever it cost.

"We're here," said Good Sister Christine.

THE NEW HEADMISTRESS

Calla had suspected that arrival at the School of the Good Sisters might be difficult, knowing how much she'd hated her old school, but she had never thought that it might involve Good Sister Christine dodging through the front door as though she was auditioning to play a ninja. It really was the strangest thing for anybody to do, let alone somebody who possessed all the nimbleness of a banana.[72]

After a second she looked back and waved to Calla. "Come on. It's safe. Quickly now. I'll take you to your room."

"Why wouldn't it be safe?" Calla wondered out loud, but Good Sister Christine was already moving back inside the building. Calla dragged her case after her and into a deserted hallway. There was no carpet on the floor, and the sound of her feet and the case was not the sound of somebody who did not wish to be noticed.

She'd barely made it halfway down the hall when a door opened and a woman appeared from the shadows before

---

72 It is a description that applies to all of us forced to wear such impracticable outfits.

them. She wore the same outfit as Good Sister Christine, but it looked completely different on her. Good Sister Christine's dress and scarf were almost part of her, but this woman wore her clothes as though they'd been in an argument and weren't talking to each other anymore. Her hair wasn't covered by the scarf at all, but rather pulled back so tightly from her face that she looked as though she was in pain. It was a curiously fitting expression.

Calla took a step back as the woman swept toward her. She really couldn't help it.

"You're late," said the woman.

"Car," said Good Sister Christine economically. "Wrench. Problems. Solved now, though. Calla really was very understanding of the situation. I think we need to enroll her in Good Sister Honey's Advanced Mechanics class."

It was when Calla watched Good Sister Christine give the woman a big smile that she realized something very particular. Good Sister Christine did not like this woman. She did not like her at all.

"We can't continue to have these situations," said the woman. "You know it's a new broom this term, Christine. Things have got to change."

"Perhaps, Headmistress," said Good Sister Christine. She gave the headmistress a big smile. It was the sort of smile that only smiled on the surface.

Calla did not like those sorts of smiles.

"There's no *perhaps* about it," said the headmistress. "We're already running late. I don't have time for this. Is this all of her luggage? But where's her trunk?"

"I don't have a trunk," said Calla. "And if I did, it wouldn't have fit in the car because of all the bo—"

"Boxes!" said Good Sister Christine quickly. "I brought back some boxes for the girls to pack things into. So we can put things into them. Yes. Things."

The headmistress gave Good Sister Christine a long and peculiarly adult look, and for the moment seemed to have forgotten Calla even existed. It was a very useful thing for her to do because Calla was staring at the papers that the headmistress held in her hand. At the top of one of the sheets, just in the corner, was a familiar symbol. A duck with its wings crossed behind its back and, just beneath it, the words *The Malus Organization*.

"What's the Malus Organization?" said Calla, unable to stop herself. "I know that name—"

The headmistress shifted the papers so quickly that Calla almost thought she'd imagined it. "One of the first things you will learn here," she said coldly, "is not to ask impertinent questions. Now. You can call me headmistress when you talk to me, or Ms. DeWitt[73] in absolute emergencies. Is that clear?"

"Okay," said Calla, and when Good Sister Christine made a *Did you not hear what she just said?* face at her, she added, "Headmistress."

"You're a quicker learner than your mother."

"Excuse me?" said Calla, unable to stop herself.

"Don't interrupt me. Courtesy is next to godliness, and you are in need of both."

....

73 Sound familiar?

Calla was rather sure that both she and her mum had just been insulted. At least twice. She wasn't quite sure what to say to any of that, and so she decided to change the subject. "Is Good Sister June around, please? She's my guardian and the reason my mum sent me here. I'd like to say hello."

"You'll be able to say hello later," said the headmistress. "My word, I can see your mother in you and I do not like what I see. You're going to have to sort yourself out."

Calla stared at her. She was appalled and fascinated in equal measure. The woman was mad. She was certain of it.

"Take her to her room, Christine," said the headmistress. "And while you're there remind them all not to be late for tonight. The whole school must be there to send *her* off in the fashion she deserves." She looked at the two of them and Calla's battered suitcase one more time. "Disgusting," she said, before marching off.

And the whole building seemed to sigh with relief.

Good Sister Christine tightened her hand on Calla's shoulder and propelled her up a nearby flight of spiral stairs that seemed to wind upward for far longer than a flight of stairs had any right to. There was a small green door at the top and just before Good Sister Christine opened it, she paused. She said, "Did you like the headmistress?" Her voice was soft and unreadable.

"I hate her," said Calla furiously.

"Well," said Good Sister Christine, "at least you're not the only one."

THE NORTH TOWER BEDROOM[74]

As anybody who has ever read a fairy tale knows, a tower is a remarkable place. It can hold mysteries, or spinning wheels, or girls with magical hair, and sometimes all three of those at once. Calla thought about all of this as she stepped through the door into the North Tower bedroom and she was not disappointed. The room was completely circular, with big and long windows cut into the walls at regular intervals, and the furniture was arranged at odd angles against the curves.

"You'll be sleeping over there," said Good Sister Christine, pointing to a neatly made bed by the window. "I'll get you some towels while I'm here and then you're good to go." She opened the nearest cupboard before closing it very swiftly. "A

....

74 There are other towers at the school (in one of which we store baked beans and bedding, in case of a very specific emergency), and they are called Tower bedrooms as well because we are imaginative about a lot of things except the naming of rooms. The North Tower bedroom is up a spiral staircase laid with green carpet, and the tower itself pokes out from the roof as though somebody was decorating a cake and had just figured out how to do a fancy thing with their icing bag. It is a perfect bedroom for mischief and tricks, and it has always been my favorite.

box of chocolates," she explained with a small smile. "If I'd seen it, then I'd have had to confiscate it under our new and delightfully restrictive rules against sugar, sweets, and generally all kinds of fun."

Calla stared at her.

"I am, however, suddenly blind," said Good Sister Christine. "Isn't it unfortunate? Make sure you have a caramel for me. Perhaps you can pray for my recovery."

As Good Sister Christine rummaged in a new cupboard and started to throw towels behind her, Calla went over to look out the window. The roofs were flat and big enough to hold a party on, and she rather thought that people had. There were scuff marks on the window ledge where somebody had climbed in and out, and the drop from the window to the roof itself was nothing more than an ambitious stretch. She'd never been out on a roof before. The idea was oddly appealing.

"Don't," said Good Sister Christine, in that startlingly acute way of hers. "The roof is all very well and good, but I have to tell you not to go on it. There is nothing there of interest, and you are here to work. Were I to tell you about the opportunities it allows to creep into each other's rooms at night, and hold midnight feasts, and to sit out and watch the sunset, and generally be where you are not expected to be, then I would be doing something very inappropriate indeed."

Calla did not know what to say to this and so she did not say anything. It was perhaps the best decision to make under the circumstances.

Good Sister Christine presented Calla with a pile of towels.

One of them was so small that it looked like it was intended for a doll. "It's a washcloth," she said.

Calla looked blank. "I don't even know what that's for."

"I've never felt older," said Good Sister Christine. "It is a cloth for your face. Every girl here has one. Wash your face with it before you go to bed. Worship the delights of a washcloth."

"Okay," said Calla. She made a mental note to never touch the tiny towel.

"Edie and Hanna will be up once afternoon school finishes, and then you can all get acquainted." There was the smallest of pauses before the nun continued. "You're all due in the dining hall for supper. They'll direct you. Make sure that you're not late. It's an important night."

"Okay," Calla said again.

"Any questions?"

Oh, Calla had plenty of questions and most of them centered on how to make the nun not leave her here, in this room, by herself.[75] Good Sister Christine seemed nice, if quite weird, and if she'd been friends with her mum then Calla could be friends with her. Calla wasn't sure she was allowed to be friends with grown-ups, or teachers, or even nuns, but this was a very weird time and she was going to take support wherever she found it.

But none of this could be said, because grown-ups were grown-ups all the world over and Good Sister Christine clearly

---

75 I have checked with Calla and she informs me that her questions were of the following nature: 1. Why Is the Headmistress Clearly Evil? 2. What Is a WASHCLOTH???? (she insisted I put the extra question marks here) and 3. Are the Girls in this Bedroom Anywhere Near as Horrible as Miranda Price?

thought that Calla was okay.[76] Her hand was already on the door, and she was pushing it open. In the distance came the sound of a bell. "That's the end of school," said Good Sister Christine, "they'll be here shortly. Are you sure you'll be all right to wait for them?"

Calla nodded. "Yes,"[77] she said, knowing that there was nothing else she could say. "I'll be brave."[78]

---

76 She thought this with some justification because "I'm okay" was, after all, the only thing Calla had said for the past ten minutes.

77 This was a lie.

78 This was not.

INTRODUCING EDMÉE AGATHE AURORE BERGER AND HANNA KOWALCZYK

After Good Sister Christine closed the door behind her, Calla really was left quite alone. It wasn't as bad as she had thought it would be. She had been alone on the train, and on the platform, and she'd survived that. As long as Miranda Price didn't walk through the door in the next five minutes, everything was going to be all right.

Almost unconsciously, Calla opened her suitcase and took out the battered mobile phone that her mum had given her. It wasn't pretty and it couldn't do anything fancy, but it was the most precious thing she had. And even though it was far too soon for Elizabeth to call as she'd still be on the plane, Calla couldn't help hoping that it would ring.

At that moment the bedroom door opened and a small girl bounced into the room. She dropped an exercise book by one bed, dropped herself onto the other, and pulled her dark hair out of its clip with a loud sigh of relief. And it was only then that she looked at Calla and said, "*Salut.* Who are you?"

"Calla," said Calla, hastily stuffing the phone back into her case.

"Calla what?" said the girl. She had a French accent that

every now and then seemed to grow more pronounced. When Calla didn't immediately reply, she said: "Calla uncomfortable silence? Calla awkward pause? It is an interesting name, I think, but I don't think it's really your name."

"Calla North," said Calla North, who was slightly dazzled by the whole encounter. "I'm new. Good Sister Christine brought me up here and told me to wait for Edie and Hanna?" She was very aware that she was babbling and so she stopped herself by biting her bottom lip. It was a painful and yet quite effective method, best to save for emergencies.

"I am Edmée Agathe Aurore Berger," said Edmée. "But you can call me Edie, because nobody but my ancient grand-mère calls me that, and she's too busy leaving her fortune to the dogs to remember that she has children, let alone grandchildren." She paused for breath. "Hanna's on her way but she's been delayed by Good Sister Paulette, who will insist on people doing their homework. I knew Hanna would forget so I offered to do it for her, as I did last term, but Hanna's developing a conscience and was determined to do it herself, and here we are. It really is most tiresome. Why are you called Calla? I've never heard of anybody being called that."

Other people might have been surprised by the sudden change of topic, or indeed the volley of information that had just been thrown at them, but Calla could deal with this sort of thing with her eyes closed. Elizabeth had never been one for linear thinking when she was excited. Neither, it seemed, was Edmée Agathe Aurore Berger. "My dad's favorite flower was a calla lily, and so that's what they called me. We put them on his grave when they're in season."

Edie nodded. "That makes sense. I'm sorry about your dad. Mine is alive, though I barely see him. He is with the army, and stationed somewhere I forget the name of. Really, it's as if I'm an orphan. My life is unbearably romantic that way."

The door opened for a second time. "Calla, meet Hanna Kowalczyk," said Edie, doing introductions as she collapsed back onto her bed. "Hanna, meet Calla North. She's new. Delightful joy."

Hanna grinned at Calla, before walking over to Edie's bed and sitting squarely on top of her. "Hi," she said to Calla, ignoring Edie's yells. "I'm so glad you're here! When term started, it was just us two, and when it got into March, I thought we weren't *ever* going to get a third roommate and we needed somebody because people were all, 'I can't tell the difference between you two' and I was like, 'Well, she's the one with the big hair and French accent and I'm the one with the glasses,' and they were all 'I still don't know' and I was—"

"Shut up," said Edie from beneath her. It was quite muffled, but still distinct. Edie was particularly talented that way.

Hanna made a surprised face and sat up, pulling Edie out from underneath her. "Sorry, I didn't see you."[79]

Edie gave her a Look before throwing a pillow at her. Hanna managed to dodge it, but the pile of clothes next to her didn't. They slid down onto the floor and a pair of socks rolled all the way over to Calla's feet.

"Throw them back at her," advised Edie, lounging on her bed.

"Ignore her," said Hanna, pushing her glasses back up her

---

79 She did. Trust me.

nose. "I have a question to ask you, Calla, and we can't go anywhere or do anything or even possibly talk to you until you answer it."

"All right," said Calla, putting down the socks. She felt just a little bit nervous all over again. "What is it?"

"What's the last book you read?" said Hanna.

"*The Breeding Habits of* Mallardus Amazonica," said Calla. "By my mum."

Hanna didn't say anything.

Edie didn't say anything.

And it was then Calla realized that that might not have been the answer that they'd been expecting.

THE IMPORTANCE OF STORIES

"Have you read any *school* stories? We know your mum's a super-author woman but that's not what I meant."

"I don't read anything like that," said Calla.

"But you must. Nobody comes to boarding school without having read school stories. You have to have read some of them at least. Enid Blyton? *The Chalet School*? Or Angela Brazil? What about Robin Stevens? Kate Saunders?"[80]

Calla shook her head.

"Okay," Hanna said desperately, "do you believe in Morally Improving books? Is that the sort of thing you read? I have to know what you think about books. You might be like *her*."

"Like *who*?" said Calla. "There's a lot of people that could mean."

Edie stood up and walked to the door. She opened it, peered down the stairs, and then closed it. "Coast is clear. Go ahead. Tell her everything she needs to know. And while you do, brush your hair so we're not late for dinner."

"The headmistress," said Hanna. She didn't move an inch.

....

80 What a list! Truly, Hanna could be terribly brilliant at times.

"This school used to be the best thing ever, but it's not. Not now. When we came back after half-term in February, everything had changed. We didn't realize it at first, but slowly it all got worse. They took away our mobile phones—"

"The official ones *and* the unofficial ones," added Edie. She looked pale at the memory. "They went through our sock drawers and everything."

"That was at the end of February."

"And now the only phone you can use is in *her* study. Literally the only phone in the entire school, and she has it locked up."

"She's made all the common rooms out of bounds. We're supposed to go straight to our bedrooms after dinner." Hanna paused for dramatic effect as she reached the most important point in her list of horror. "And she's even changed the *menu*."

"That doesn't sound so bad," said Calla, who was used to eating whatever was on offer that week, regardless of how well it went together.

"You've never had rainbow sponge and chocolate custard. Good Sister Honey is, like, the best cook ever, and we all worship her. She's basically a wizard. But with scones."

Edie wrinkled her nose in disgust. "And now she has to make things like Brussels sprouts cake and spirulina smoothies and kale milkshakes."

"That wasn't so bad when we still had cookery classes."

"But now we don't even have them. She's canceled cookery, and drama, and art, and camping out in the woods and ballroom dancing and fencing and helicopter maintenance[81]—"

....

81 Good Sister Honey is an excellent pilot.

"What?" said Calla, wondering if she'd heard this correctly. "You do all of those?"

Hanna nodded. "We did," she said, "but that was under Good Sister June. She was our old headmistress, but the school's been bought out by a big company and the new school board said we weren't getting good enough grades so they shipped *her* in. She used to be a pupil here or something. Like that makes it better."

"I'm going to make her life hell," Edie murmured dreamily.

"Edie has powers in that direction. Usually she uses them for good, but I have authorized her to use them to get rid of the headmistress. Whatever it takes. It was when—when she got rid of the fiction in the library. All of the boarding school stories. That was it. That was when I knew. She got rid of everything good and brilliant and replaced it with books about—about *algebra*."

"Oh my god," said Calla.[82]

"Precisely," said Edie. She glanced at the clock on the wall and let out a small, ineffably chic gasp. "We need to take her to the Hall, Hanna, or we shall be late for dinner."

"Do we go the normal way or the . . . other ways?"[83] said Hanna. There was a subtle pause that really was not quite as subtle as she had intended it to be.

Edie embraced a rare moment of tactfulness and pretended to not notice. "The normal way," she said, ignoring the *What*

----

82 Quite an understandable reaction under the circumstances. I am no fan of algebra myself. In fact, I am not fond of most math unless it can help me work out the appropriate jam-to-cream ratio on a freshly baked scone.

83 This will not make much sense to you now, but later it will. Trust me.

on earth are you on about? look Calla was currently giving her. "For now. We'll introduce her to the other ones soon. Anyway, look—come on. We have to get moving before one of our beloved prison guards comes to get us."

And so they moved. Hanna held the door open, and Edie grabbed Calla's hand and pulled her down the stairs. The three of them ran through the deserted entrance hallway before skidding to the left and down a long, dark corridor. They passed windows that looked out onto a yard where vegetables grew alongside a long-forgotten duck house, and locked common rooms that ached for company, and then all of a sudden, into a corridor that was full of girls. They were everywhere and Calla, who had not dealt with girls well ever since Miranda Price had picked her last for basketball and then spent the game throwing the ball directly at her head, felt a little bit panicky at the sight and started to slow down.

It can be understood that Edie and Hanna felt no such qualms. It can also be understood that Edie was not the sort of person to let a new girl navigate such complicated waters by herself. She kept her hand wrapped around Calla's and pulled her into a gap in the line. Hanna slid in neatly behind them, and as the three of them caught their breath and tried to look as though they had been there all along, a man appeared in the distance.

Both Edie and Hanna stiffened, as did the girls around them. It was not that a man was surprising, for men do exist and some of them are rather lovely and make an excellent Battenberg, but the fact that one had appeared in a girls' boarding school was very surprising indeed.

The man was enormously tall and looked deeply uncomfortable.[84] None of the nuns in the corridor spoke to him or even seemed to notice him. They were too busy walking in and out of the dining room and whispering to each other under their breath. Calla found herself watching them as much as she watched the man. Not one nun looked happy, or even pleased to be there, and that was curious. Something had happened or, perhaps, was happening even now.

The headmistress appeared at the end of the corridor. She was surrounded by more men, all of them wearing the same dark-colored suit as the gigantic man who had been there all along. It was the sort of dark-colored suit that people wore when they did not wish to be noticed.

Calla had seen people like this before. They'd last come when she'd worn her old school uniform for so long that the holes had started to develop holes. They were in the house one evening when she got home, and while one stayed in the kitchen and talked to Elizabeth, the others took Calla aside for a Private Chat. They'd told her that her mum wasn't able to look after her right now, and that there were other people who could help. They'd never understood that Calla could deal with anything providing she had her mum at her side.

Suited people were problems.

But a more pressing problem was the fact that Hanna was elbowing her in her ribs and saying, "Pay attention."

....

84 As I imagine you would, were you being observed by a cabal of inquisitive girls. Poor Gareth. He really did have a lot to put up with. You'll learn more about him shortly.

Calla pulled herself away from her thoughts and paid attention.

"This is Rose Bastable," said Hanna, gesturing at a girl their age. She had her hair pulled back into intricate braids that made Calla instantly envious of her. Her own bright yellow hair did nothing but stand up like a thick and unruly bush however many times she brushed it. "Rose, this is Calla. She's named after a plant too. She's new and in our bedroom."

"Poor you," said Rose sweetly. "Edie can be *trop difficile* to cope with."

"Not compared to you," Hanna said loyally. "I still haven't forgotten that time you cried when Sister Honey put raisins in the cookies instead of chocolate."[85]

"I was six," began Rose, but then she stopped. Good Sister Christine was standing in the doorway and clapping her hands together for their attention.

"Girls," said Good Sister Christine. She caught Calla's eye and gave her a brief thumbs-up before she stepped back. "You can go in now," she said. "Quickly, please."

---

85 To be fair to Rose, raisins in cookies can be really quite unfortunate.

IN WHICH CALLA MEETS SOMEBODY VERY IMPORTANT

The dining hall was twice as big as the biggest room that Calla had ever been in, and had more paintings on the wall than they had in their entire house.[86] It was also full of twice as many girls as Calla had ever seen, and a high proportion of those looked like they could be Miranda Price. She took a deep breath and sat where Edie told her to sit and tried to ignore how there were at least four different forks laid out in front of her.

"Do not worry about the cutlery," said Edie, who had, of course, noticed Calla's slight panic. "Work from the outside in. It is part of the headmistress's new ideas to make us good little girls."

"Good little girls from the 1900s," said Rose from farther down their table. "How does knowing which fancy fork to use when make us better?"

Hanna grinned. "I've been to enough government dinners

---

86 Admittedly that was zero paintings, because Elizabeth had long since sold everything that she could sell, but that was not the point.

to know that it doesn't matter," she said, "but some stupid people like to think it does."

"Good Sister June never cared about any of this stuff," Rose said morosely. "We absolutely have to *do something* about this."

Edie was about to respond, but then she stopped because the food was arriving. It was served by a series of nuns who looked absolutely furious with the world. They put their dishes down on the table before returning to sit with the rest of the staff in grim, severe silence.

Calla could barely focus on her meal,[87] and instead found herself studying the nuns and trying to figure out what was happening. They all kept looking at one woman in particular. She was a nun, older than Good Sister Christine, with pale white hair that curled out from underneath her scarf. She was not what you would call pretty, and indeed she had not been called pretty at many points in her life, but she was the sort of person that you would look at twice.

Calla knew, as clearly as if she'd been told, that this was Good Sister June.

And Good Sister June was staring right back at her.

---

[87] Boiled sardines, with mung bean mash. Horrific, isn't it? I had to have a slice of Victoria sponge just to get over the thought.

THE DIFFICULTIES OF STARING
AT STRANGERS

Calla North did not know Good Sister June one bit and so when Good Sister June looked at her in a *Something's Up and I Know That and I Am Trying to Solve It Golly Don't You Look Like Just Your Mother* sort of fashion, Calla simply looked back at her in an *I Don't Have the Slightest Clue What You're Saying but I'm Sure It's Fascinating* manner.

Good Sister June stood up and pushed her chair back under her table. She took a step toward where Calla sat.

Just one.

And then she stopped, and an instant later Calla realized why. The headmistress had stood and was clapping for attention, and the whole room looked up expectantly. It was time for the speeches, and nobody was going to get to talk to anybody else until they were done.

However much they needed to.

LADIES AND SMALLER LADIES, YOUR ATTENTION, PLEASE

The headmistress walked all the way around the table until she stood in between Good Sister Christine and Good Sister June.

"We are all here tonight to say thank you to somebody very important to us all," she said, resting her hand on Good Sister June's shoulder. "I've known Good Sister June ever since I was a pupil at this school myself. She's changed so many lives and made so many people who they are today. And now we must say goodbye to her."

She paused for the room to applaud. The suited men clapped, but none of the girls or the nuns moved an inch. The headmistress did not seem to notice this. "I am so humbled[88] to be here in front of you now, to guide you all through the coming months. Tonight, however, we pay tribute to the past." The headmistress lingered just a little too long on that final word. "Good Sister June is retiring. She has been a splendid Head but the time has come for her to move on.

---

88 Of all the complex things she was, I can assure you that Magda DeWitt has never been remotely humble.

She'll still be on site, of course, as she will be working in our convent. Your daily contact with her will be little to none. It's for the best, really. It's time the school had a strong and stable headmistress as opposed to somebody who makes the rules up as they go along. Or who changes things to suit *certain students* and not others. Favoritism shall no longer be tolerated."

Good Sister Christine looked up at that. Calla had the strangest thought that she was going to say something, but she didn't. She looked at Good Sister June who, almost imperceptibly, shook her head. Calla only noticed it because she was staring straight at her.

"There are going to be changes. There will be no time now for frivolous extracurricular activities. There will be no ridiculous desserts like rainbow sponge and custard. Your work will be suitably challenging, and if any of you are caught helping each other with homework, there will be *consequences*."

The headmistress's speech continued, but Calla could barely pay attention to what was being said, because she had just noticed something. The strange men in suits all had a logo stitched onto their jacket pockets. A duck, with its wings crossed behind its back, and the letters *M.O.* The same logo she had seen on the papers in the headmistress's hand earlier that afternoon. The same logo that she was sure she'd seen before.

A silence in the hall snapped Calla back to attention. The headmistress had paused, and smiled another one of those awfully strange smiles of hers. "My goodness. I believe

I've spoken for far too long. I'm so sorry, girls, but that means we don't have time for speeches from anybody else. Perhaps we should finish the night there—"

Good Sister Christine pushed her chair back and stood up. "Nobody's going anywhere," she said. "Not yet."

THE SECOND (AND MOST IMPORTANT) SPEECH

"I'd like to say a few words," said Good Sister Christine. She did not wait for the headmistress to reply. In fact, she did not even look at her. She got up from the table and turned so that she had her back to the men in suits and didn't see how they looked at her, and then at the headmistress, and how one of them even got up to say something, before sitting down very quickly as an elderly nun glared ferociously at him.[89]

Calla had the sneaking suspicion that even if Good Sister Christine had seen this, she wouldn't have stopped speaking. She had a very determined expression on her face, just like Elizabeth did when she had a deadline and the promise of payment.

"Good Sister June means the world to me," said Good Sister Christine. "To all of us. I promise you that even if we can't talk to her, she will still be here. Even if she's in the convent with the other praying sisters, she'll still be our headmistress. Always."

One by one the girls in the hall started to applaud, until the

....

89 This was Good Sister Gwendolyn. She really can be most ferocious at times.

116

sound filled the room entirely. Calla thought she saw Hanna wiping a tear from her eye.

Good Sister June placed her hand on Good Sister Christine's arm. She rose, just a little, and murmured something into the younger nun's ear. Good Sister Christine shook her head. Good Sister June nodded and then sat back down. Her hand, however, stayed on Good Sister Christine's arm.

Calla watched all of this with a frown. She had watched adults all her life. She had watched them tell her the truth and she had watched them tell her lies. And right now, it looked as though there was a very big lie going on. She just couldn't figure out whose or what it was.

The headmistress coughed. Loudly.

The clapping faded into silence.

"It's all yours," said Good Sister Christine. "Thank you *so* much, Headmistress."

AN ENDING AND A BEGINNING, TOO

The headmistress left the room the moment Good Sister Christine had finished speaking. She was swiftly followed by most of the men in suits before one, the gigantic man that Calla had noticed before the party, came back in and sat next to one of the smaller nuns. He began to talk to her as though nothing out of the ordinary was happening.[90]

For a moment, nobody else moved, until suddenly everybody got up at once. The bigger girls began to help the nuns tidy up, whilst the younger girls seized the sudden freedom and began to chat loudly among themselves. Edie, Rose, and Hanna began a fierce argument that didn't make much sense to anybody at their table but somehow involved all of them. All of them except for Calla, who pushed back her chair and started to walk toward the staff table. She wanted to speak to Good Sister June before she disappeared. She had to. The nun

....

90   And as far as Gareth knew, it wasn't. Gareth had been doing his job, and now that the headmistress was on her way back to the study, he had some free time to ask Good Sister Honey about how to make her cheese scones. His heart has always been in baked goods, and Good Sister Honey's scones are remarkable things. The secret is mustard.

was the nearest thing she had to her mum, and she didn't want to let her disappear.

Good Sister June seemed to be on a similar mission. She began to work through the crowd of girls toward Calla in a most determined sort of fashion. She paused only to smile at people and tell them that everything would be all right and she would be back soon.[91] When she eventually reached Calla and the two of them stared at each other in the way that people do when they have so much they want to say that they don't even know where to begin, Good Sister Christine tried to fill in the gap. She said, "June, there's somebody I need to introduce you to—"

"That's not necessary," said Good Sister June. A small smile creased across her sad face and completely transformed her. "Hello, Calla."

---

[91] This was not the sort of thing that people tended to say at retirement parties, but, as you have probably gathered, this was no normal retirement party.

THE PROMISE OF GOOD SISTER JUNE

"Hello," said Calla.

"You look so much like Elizabeth," said Good Sister June. "It's the hair. Your eyes, too. All of you. Everything." She seemed both surprised and comforted by it. "Have you heard from her yet? I understand that communications will be difficult."

Calla nodded. "She'll be on a plane now. I'm not sure which one. But when she lands in South America, it'll be tomorrow night and that's when she'll ring me." The moment that she finished speaking, she remembered that all the phones in the school had been confiscated and went bright red. "I don't have a phone," she said, trying desperately to cover her tracks. "It's just—I don't. I don't know why I said I did."

"Don't worry," said Good Sister June. She glanced behind her. "Your mother told me she was sending you with a phone. I'm glad she did. Make sure you keep it somewhere safe. You might need it sooner than you think. Things aren't quite right here at the moment, and I'd like to tell you more about that but I don't think I have time. I wanted to warn your mother, but I didn't realize how wrong things were until it was already too late. Just listen to me. You might find it difficult to believe right now, but this school is the best place I've ever known, and I'm going to get it back. I just need to find something to convince the new governors and right now, they've been dazzled by Magda and her wealthy backers. All those people quoting *numbers* and *results*. No wonder their heads have been turned. They're believing her lies."

"I don't understand," said Calla slowly. "Don't you want to go?"

"Why would I leave the best job I've ever had?" said Good Sister June. She smiled, but she didn't look happy. In fact, Calla rather thought she looked furious.[92] "I'm being made to leave, Calla, but I'll come back. I just have to prove the case against Magda. Find some evidence that she's up to something. Something that they'll believe. And until then, I can't stay here."

"But you're my guardian—"

"And I'll always be that. If you need me, you just get word to me. Send me a signal. We might not be allowed phones, but the convent isn't far away. And the moment that you need me, I'll come running. But until then, you look to Good Sister Christine. She'll help you when I can't."[93]

Upon hearing her name, Good Sister Christine leaned over.

....

92 She was.

93 It may be understood between you and me that Good Sister June's emotions were about to get the better of her. This is why, after she finished speaking, she looked away and found something very interesting on the wall to study. It is how adults deal with things. It's not necessarily the best way to deal with things, but it's what we do.

"We're running out of time," she said softly. "Good Sister Honey's stalling but I don't know how long she can keep it up."

"All right," said Good Sister June. She fixed her big, sharp eyes on Calla's face. "I'm going to sort this out. All of it. You just need to hold on until then."

And if there was one thing that Calla North knew, it was that she knew how to hold on.

She had, after all, been doing it all her life.

"Okay," she said. "All right."

THE FIRST MORNING

On her first full morning at the School of the Good Sisters, Calla opened her eyes and thought about her mum. Elizabeth had been in this very school, and maybe slept in this very bedroom. She'd had a midnight feast on top of one of the flat roofs.[94] She'd rescued injured ducks and released them back into the wild. She'd even passed an exam or two. And she would be making her first phone call tonight to Calla, and everything would be all right.

Even if the school was full of weirdness.

She rolled over and dug into her suitcase. It was still packed, the clothes piled on top of each other in a sort of "let's hope for the best" fashion. Calla had the sneaking suspicion that one of the nuns might have issues with that (tidiness is a peculiarly adult concern) and so she told herself to sort it out. But first she needed to check her phone and put it somewhere safe. The memory of accidentally confessing

---

94 "Anchovy sandwiches," said Elizabeth with delight. "Anchovy sandwiches are hideous things, but at midnight, outside, on a roof, they are the most perfect thing in existence."

everything to Good Sister June last night was still very present in Calla's thoughts.

She found her phone next to a spare pair of socks and underneath another pair of socks. She pulled it out and hid it underneath her bed, pushing it to the side that was farthest away from the door and up against the wall. For good measure, she threw the socks on the floor in front of it to distract anybody who got that far. The phone would be safe. And when she had finished all of that, a bell began to ring.

Reacting more on instinct than on actually being awake (a skill that every boarding school student develops sooner rather than later), Hanna bounced to her feet. She began to get dressed and even though her eyes were still very definitely shut and she was currently trying to put her socks on her head, she was being substantially more productive than Edie. Edie Berger hadn't even moved yet despite the very loud bell, the fact that Hanna was now falling over more than she was getting dressed, and the fact that the school was almost buzzing with noise. All of the other bedrooms, especially the ones they could see from their windows, had people getting dressed in them. Some of them were more dressed than others, and several looked to be in the middle of a healthy pillow fight, but they were all up.

Everybody except Edie, who was now, in fact, snoring.

As she studied her, Calla became convinced that it wasn't a real-life snore. Another part of her, however, rather admired Edie's commitment to her sleep. She decided to get dressed and if Edie was still in bed by the time she had her new uniform on, then Calla would accidentally-on-purpose drop something loud and heavy next to her bed. The thought was immensely satisfying.

Calla leaned back down to her case and tried to find her school uniform. Her old school had insisted on green everything for their uniform. A green tie, and a green blazer, and green shorts for PE. It wasn't even a good green,[95] but in comparison to this uniform, it was perfect. The School of the Good Sisters clearly liked their students to look like something out of Victorian times.[96] It was awful. The shirt was scratchy and the collar too high, and the dark gray skirt was far too long. Calla felt as though she was a hundred years old.

Hanna opened one eye. "The uniform's horrible. I mean, it looks fine until you get it on. If it makes you feel any better, you end up getting used to it. I felt awful the first time I put it on but I don't even think about it now."

"How long have you been here?"

"Four years," said Hanna. She opened her other eye and started to head toward the door. "All of them have been perfect, but not this one. Not with *her* in charge."

"She won't last," said a new voice. "I am going to make her leave. I am decided." It was Edie. Who was now, somehow, completely dressed.

. . . .

95 I am reliably, if somewhat crudely, informed that it was a "snot green." And not the sort of snot green that's nice, the sort of snot that you get after thirteen weeks of being ill. My apologies for the detail, but I think it's only fair that you suffer just as I have.

96 I think this is a tad unfair, but Calla has insisted on this being reported verbatim. This is what she thought and so it goes in, and even though I think she's being somewhat hyperbolic, she's very persuasive.

Calla blinked. "How did you—?"

"You look like a fancy-dress sad person," Edie said to Calla, ignoring her question. "Like a sad, sad person who has been forced to eat broccoli for breakfast."

"She's wearing the exact same clothes as you," said Hanna.

"I am used to the sadness," said Edie. "But it will not last. Once I am done, we will lose the headmistress, and Good Sister June will come back and we will sort out everything. Even this awful uniform they are so fond of. I promise you. I will sort all of this out."

"She's not joking," Hanna said to Calla. "She's actually pretty serious."

"I get that," said Calla, staring at Edie with fascination. She'd never met anybody like her. The girl burned with energy. Calla had the curious sensation that it was not the sort of energy that she ever wanted to get on the wrong side of.

Edie smiled at the two of them benevolently. "My reign of terror shall begin after breakfast," she said, heading toward the door. "A meal for which, my friends, we are already late."

A DAY LIKE NO OTHER

Edie was not wrong. They were late for breakfast and even though it was the sort of breakfast that you wanted to be late for,[97] they were unfortunately on time enough to get a substantial helping. Calla ate her toast in grim silence and thought about what she would tell her mum that evening. She was not sure that she would tell her the truth[98] and so she was figuring out what she would say instead. She eventually settled on telling her that she was all right and that she missed her and that she loved her as much as she loved the last biscuit in the tin. None of these three things were a lie, and they were not quite the complete truth,[99] and so they would do.

And then she stopped thinking about that because she had to think about surviving her first day at the School of the Good Sisters. Any first day anywhere is a difficult thing, but Calla's first day here was more complicated than normal. Not only did she have to navigate a completely new school and timetable

---

97 Mackerel fillets and sprouted seeds, with rye toast and organic peanut butter.

98 What good would it have done under the circumstances?

99 "The school is super weird and I sort of maybe want to come home."

(with completely new people, every one of them a potential Miranda Price), but she also had to navigate the oppressive presence of the headmistress. She was everywhere and even a sudden plague of stink bombs[100] did not distract her.

Calla's first lesson was science. This was with a nun called Good Sister Paulette, who spent the first fifteen minutes of the lesson talking about How to Put a Brave Face on Things.[101] Good Sister Paulette was trying very hard to toe the line with the new regime, although she did pause to surreptitiously slip Edie a list of notes on how she could improve her stink-bomb-building technique. Once she had finished encouraging the revolution, Good Sister Paulette launched into a fierce lecture about the difference between mass and density. When she had finished, she dictated five nearly impossible questions to be answered for homework before sweeping majestically out of the room. All of the girls stared at each other in shock. Calla was fairly sure that at least three of them were trying not to cry.

"This is all because of the headmistress," Edie said darkly. She pushed her chair back and walked to the front of the room, and even though she was barely tall enough to be seen

....

100 This is not a euphemism for a fart. Edie had been busy overnight in the laboratory putting together several items for her campaign against the headmistress and the first of these were stink bombs. They smelled a little bit of stinky socks, rotten eggs, and spoiled milk, and were very effective. I was not sorry to miss them.

101 Normally I am not comfortable with putting random capital letters in the middle of a sentence, but this was the sort of statement that required them.

over the heads of the front row, she commanded everybody's attention. "I am going to get rid of her," she said. "Let me tell you how."

Hanna, who was possessed of a certain amount of common sense, got up and pushed the door shut. Edie gave her a quick nod of approval before continuing.

"I am going to get rid of the headmistress, and anybody who wishes to join me can. It will be dangerous, and will involve us breaking the law at many points and perhaps one of us might die, but it will be a noble death and definitely worth it."

The girls started to talk among themselves and Edie smiled with satisfaction. She gestured up at the board. "A gift to affirm my good intentions in this matter," she said. "The answer to question number three is forty-two."

IN WHICH THINGS GO FROM BAD TO WORSE

Calla lost her ruler somewhere between science and English, and when she had to underline all of the abstract nouns[102] in a passage about kale, she had to use her index finger and hope for the best. The "best" saw a lot of pen on her finger, not much on the exercise book, and Edie offering her a replacement ruler. Unfortunately Edie did this when they were supposed to be working silently. What's more, she did it at quite a loud volume—one might say, the sort of volume you would use on a ship in the middle of a force-ten gale—and there is a lot that Good Sister Gwendolyn can ignore, but a bellowing Edmée Berger is not one of them. Good Sister Gwendolyn drew herself up to the full extent of her four feet nothing,[103] and told Edie she was an impertinent, recalcitrant, and contumacious individual. Edie was not 100 percent sure whether this was a compliment or not[104] and so, when Good Sister Gwendolyn had asked her what she thought about this, she

---

102 Honestly, nobody knows what these are.

103 A feat she had not achieved for the past five years due to a particularly determined spell of lumbago.

104 It was not.

replied quite honestly that she did not know what to think, as she hadn't understood any of it. This had resulted in a lot more yelling from the pocket-size nun and Calla and Edie being given enough lines to keep them writing for the next ten years.[105]

As Calla filed dazedly out of the classroom, Edie pulled her aside. "I'm sorry—I did not mean for that to happen. I will do your lines for you, if you want."

"It's not your fault."

"It kind of is her fault a little," said Hanna as she came over to join them. "But I think it's the headmistress's fault more. She's changed *everything*. Good Sister Gwendolyn used to be amazing. She used to spend her days reading in the library and when they got rid of the sofas, she had nowhere else to go so she came and taught. And now she's so angry all the time."

They began to walk down toward the hall for lunch. Calla didn't recognize where she was until all of a sudden she saw the familiar corridors and walls from yesterday. They walked past several of the nuns having frantic conversations in their classrooms, and came across the tall man from before having a conversation with Good Sister Paulette about scones.

"Do you think it's jam before cream or cream before jam?" He looked thoughtful before a wide, bright smile slid across his face. "Honestly, it's all the same, isn't it? You just want the whole lovely thing at once, don't you." Good Sister Paulette

---

105 "I will not come to a lesson unprepared."

looked at him and said something that Calla couldn't hear. It seemed to satisfy the man because he laughed and wandered off happily in the opposite direction. Good Sister Paulette stood there for a moment before walking purposefully after him.

"Who is that man?" said Calla, gesturing.

The other girls shrugged. "He turned up with the new head," said Hanna, "and he's really into baked goods. I keep seeing him talking to Good Sister Honey about recipes, so that means he's all right.[106] I think. I mean, nobody even knows his name."[107]

She glanced over at Edie, but Edie was busy talking to a small first-year. They watched her give the child a package before ushering her off.

"Well?" said Hanna when Edie came back to join them.

"It begins tonight," said Edie.[108] "The first-years are installing a beeper just outside of the headmistress's bedroom. It's going to go off at one in the morning and get increasingly louder until she won't be able to sleep a wink. And the best thing is, she won't be able to find it unless she lifts the floorboard by her door. It turns out Ellen has *impeccable* carpentry skills."

....

106 In the eyes of Hanna, nobody who enjoys baked goods can be a bad person. She is Not Wrong with this, though there is an exception for those people who like eccles cakes and nothing else. They are not the best sort of people.

107 I do. He's called Gareth. He's actually quite pleasant, though he is—at this point in the story—making a lot of bad decisions.

108 Technically it had begun earlier that morning with the stink bombs, but we shall not deny Edie the use of a Dramatic Phrase.

"Amazing," said Calla.

Edie smiled at her. "I promised a revolution," she said. "This is just the beginning."

And when Edmée Berger made a promise, she really did make it for keeps.

A MIDNIGHT TRIP OVER THE ROOFS

That night, Edie led the members of the North Tower bedroom across the roofs at midnight. She informed them of certain rules before doing so[109] and then climbed out the window and said, "Follow me." And when you are presented at midnight with a small, determined French girl telling you to follow her, you do precisely that. Hanna was already halfway out the window by the time Calla had figured out what was going on and then when she did, she joined the two of them on the roof and felt her heart almost explode from excitement. She didn't usually do things like this. But now she did, and it was perfect.

Hanna gestured at the moon and stars above them and said, "We used to do this actually officially. Good Sister June took us all out here once for an evening performance of some theatre thing the little kids had been working on. Good Sister Honey brought cupcakes. We stayed out here until the sun came up."

Even in the darkness, Calla could see that Hanna was near tears. She leaned over and grabbed her hand and squeezed it.

....
109 Number one being: Do not fall off.

"Good Sister June's trying to solve this," she said. "She said she'd come back. And I know she will. It's going to get better."

"It's getting better right now," said Edie. "Or at least, it will if those *enfants* are on schedule. Come on." She gestured toward a distant window and started walking. There was just enough light to see where they were putting their feet, and Hanna paused to make sure that Calla was all right when they came to anywhere difficult. It was really just like walking down a street but this street was level with the tops of the trees, and every now and then the wind would rise enough to lift Calla's hair up off her neck and make her skin tingle with cold.

When they reached the window, Edie tapped on it three times. There was no response. She then tapped on it another three times and when there was still no response, she gave up and said, "We are here, my little *pomme de terre*. Let us in."

A small face appeared at the window. In truth, it was more eyes than face, and more panic than action. Edie could sometimes be very intimidating and her arrival at the window at midnight had panicked many people in the past. Amelia Warren was no exception to this rule and so she stood there for a moment, paralyzed by indecision, until Edie gestured at the lock on the window and raised her eyebrows pointedly. Amelia squeaked and unlocked the window, pushing it open so that the other three could climb in.

"Sorry," she said, "but I'm not good under pressure."

"You will learn," Edie said as she clambered inside the bedroom.

"We brought biscuits," said Hanna, following her. "And a new girl. This is Calla."

Calla closed the window behind her. "Hello," she said, staring with interest at the new bedroom. It was very similar to the North Tower bedroom but substantially less tidy. In fact, it looked a little bit like Amelia shared her room with a whirlwind and a cyclone and not, as she did, with a girl named Ellen and another one called Gajal. Of course Calla did not know this then, but she discovered it within the next five minutes when they returned and informed Edie that it was done. The moment that they'd finished speaking, Amelia turned off the lights, Gajal opened the curtains, and Ellen pushed the window back open.

The sound of distant beeping came across the rooftop. And then: yelling.

"Oh, well done," said Edie.

THE FIRST PROBLEM

And so, because of the night that she spent in the other bedroom and the fact that they did not get back to the North Tower until the distant sky turned pink with the dawn, Calla did not realize that her mother had not yet called her.

REALIZING AN ABSENCE IN
THE WORLD

It was not the missing of the phone call that was the problem, for Elizabeth had missed phone calls before. She was not good at doing things that had been arranged, or responding to emails on time, or indeed doing any of the things that adults expect of one another in order to maintain their adultish ways.

It was not necessarily a problem that she had missed this particular call, for there were several Important Factors to Consider. Elizabeth was excited. She was off to the Amazon. She was, in fact, there already and trying to find the duck she'd dreamed of all her life. She would check in soon enough. Everything was all right.

At least, this is what Calla told herself when she realized that her mother had not called.

I do not think she believed much of what she told herself but, at least, she tried.

THE SECRETS OF GOOD SISTER CHRISTINE

I am pleased, in a way, that all of this drama happened while Calla was at school. I appreciate that none of it would have happened at all had she stayed at home with Elizabeth in their increasingly fragile existence, but it happened and she was surrounded by friends as it did. That meant that rather than worrying about her mum, as she had done so often in the past, she had things to distract her. The first of these distractions came very early in the morning upon the second day. Unfortunately Calla was still lying in bed trying to persuade herself that everything was okay and was so lost in her thoughts that she did not notice it until Hanna squeaked in a loud and not terribly subtle sort of fashion.

Hanna's squeaks have never been the sort of thing that you could ignore, and so Calla didn't. She rolled over and beheld the curious sight of Good Sister Christine, Hanna, and Edie having a very quiet and very secretive conversation in the door of the North Tower bedroom.

A part of Calla did not move. Another part of her did not even breathe.

Good Sister Christine produced a small book from a bag she

carried on her shoulder. She gave it to Hanna and murmured something, smilingly, under her breath. Hanna squeaked again with excitement and then with annoyance when Edie elbowed her in the ribs. "Shut up," said Edie. "Calla's asleep."

Calla decided to get straight to the point. "No I'm not. What's going on?"

All three of them turned around. Hanna's turning around was rather more dramatic than the others as it involved her making a panicked expression and flinging her book to the side of the room. She then looked appalled at her actions and ran after it, apologizing under her breath.[110]

"What you have witnessed, Calla, is a secret library," said Edie with commendable and characteristic calm. "The head-mistress banned us from having good books, or actually any books at all, so Good Sister Christine brings them round first thing in the morning. She's part of the revolution. She will lead us over the barricades when the time comes."

Good Sister Christine pulled an *I'm not sure about that* face. "I'm not sure about that," she said. "I just like people to have good books." She gave Hanna a quick glance of sympathy[111] before she stepped into the North Tower bedroom and

. . . .

110 You should not fling books. You may yell at them and call them names and weep into their pages, but you should never use them as a projectile. Hanna knew this as well as the next person but the moment had put her under some pressure. She cannot be completely blamed.

111 For Hanna was currently kneeling on the floor, cradling a copy of *The Silver Brumby* to her chest and whispering a frantic apology. *The Silver Brumby* is the sort of book you should apologize to, for it is magical and perfect in every way.

carefully closed the door behind her. "We can speak freely for a while. The headmistress didn't get much sleep last night so she's resting in bed until this afternoon. Nevertheless, it does us good to take precautions under the circumstances."

Calla suddenly realized something. "This is why you had the books in the car and shushed me when I was going to mention them to *her*."

Good Sister Christine nodded. There was no need to specify who *her* was. "People who tell you what not to read are generally not good people," she said. She perched on the end of Calla's bed and patted Hanna supportively on the shoulder. Edie had already taken the opportunity to go back to sleep. "The authorities that now run this school are determined to tell you all what you should or shouldn't read and their decisions are valid, up to a point. But you cannot exist on math papers and old exams alone. You have to read some good stuff."

"Like this," said Hanna, who was now holding her book in her arms in the manner of a person who had just won the lottery.

"After you've finished that, I'll bring you *My Friend Flicka* and *Misty of Chincoteague*."

Hanna made an indescribable sound of happiness.

"I'll take that as a yes," said Good Sister Christine.

"But what if you get caught doing this?" said Calla. The thought of Good Sister Christine being caught made her feel a tiny bit sick. There was always somebody out there waiting for people to slip up. It always happened. "Will they try to get rid of you, as well?"

Good Sister Christine pulled a thoughtful expression. It was a rare and beautiful thing for her to do. She has not always been one for considering the ramifications of her actions but trust me, she'd thought this one through.

"There's a saying," she said slowly, "that you 'keep your friends close but your enemies closer.' And if I ran this school and had a hundred nuns doing what I'm doing, then I'd keep them all right where I could see them. I'm not going anywhere."

And the moment that she finished, the bell rang to start another day at the School of the Good Sisters.

THE LENGTH OF A DISTRACTION

Calla's first class took place on top of the roof. They learned how to calculate the ratio of jam-to-cream on a scone, and worked out fractions based on slices of Victoria sponge, and looked very carefully innocent when the headmistress came out to join them. If you were to look up a picture of *angry* in the dictionary, you would probably see a photograph of the expression on her face. It was not pleasant. "Why on earth are you taking your class on the roof?" she said.

"Because all of the furniture is here," said Good Sister Gwendolyn, looking rather confused. It was a very logical response really. She had been scheduled to teach a class and she could not do that without tables and chairs, so she had taken the students to where the tables and chairs were. And that was on the roof.[112]

The headmistress did not say anything.

---

112 It turns out that all you need to get furniture onto the roof are several very excitable first-years, the promise of free lemon drizzle cake for all concerned, and a solid knowledge of winches and pulleys. It is especially fortunate that these are all the sorts of things that the curriculum at the School of the Good Sisters encourages.

Good Sister Gwendolyn tried to improve the situation. I am not sure this was the best thing to do under the circumstances, but they were circumstances that required some sort of doing something. She was, after all, teaching on a roof. "The girls show an intrinsic motivation when learning in the fresh air. I read about it in one of the educational journals you made us read." The class nodded even though the vast majority of them did not understand what *intrinsic* meant, and the fresh air had actually made Rose fall asleep at her desk.

The headmistress said something that I shall not repeat here. Luckily enough she said it at a volume to wake Rose and make her hold up her hand and look like an eager member of the class.

Good Sister Gwendolyn kept her eyes on the headmistress and said, very softly, "I am teaching the girls to the best of my ability and I know that is something you want to support."

"Of course," said the headmistress. "I am here for their education above all things." It was an effort, but the headmistress said it because she knew that Good Sister Gwendolyn was right. Learning outside makes you understand things better, and focus more,[113] and sometimes when you are able to learn on a roof so high that it feels like you are more sky than person, it makes you feel like you can take on the world. The headmistress's problem was not that they were learning on the roof, but that they were doing so without permission.

And so the headmistress climbed down from the roof and

---

113 When the fresh air hasn't sent you to sleep.

went to google things like *How do I lock windows?* and Good Sister Gwendolyn went back to teaching her class.

At the end of it, however, she caught Edie and pulled her aside. "I am not making any comments nor accusing anybody of anything," she said, "but if I were the sort of person to put all of the classroom furniture on the roof overnight, I would make sure I included a comfy chair for the teacher to sit on and at least two biscuits for them to dunk into their tea."

"Custard creams?" said Edie.

"Pink wafers," said Good Sister Gwendolyn.

ANOTHER MISSED CALL

I would like you to imagine something you want very much. It doesn't matter what it is. It just matters how you feel about it. It must be one of those perfect things that will make your life a little bit better when it happens and it is so perfect that the moments leading up to it barely exist because you are just waiting for that thing to happen.

Now I would like you to imagine how you would feel if that thing does not happen.

This is precisely how Calla North felt when Elizabeth missed her second scheduled call. What was worse was that she did not answer when Calla dialed her number three times in a row. Instead, Elizabeth's voicemail answered and even the sound of her mother saying, *"Do you know what it's called when it starts raining ducks?*[114] *I'll tell you when I call you quack. Leave a message!"* did not make her feel better.

If anything, it made her feel worse.

. . . .

114 Fowl weather.

AN UNFORTUNATE REALITY

And the worst thing of all was this: Calla North had to keep going. She had to go to bed and wake up and attend school, because that was what her life was now. In a way, it is good that she had that structure about her for I think that without it, she may have curled up into a corner and begun to cry and never stop.

But that was not an option, and so she did not take it. She was brave, and every time she looked at her phone, she closed her eyes and willed her mother to call home.

And every now and then, a revolution led by a small and quite furious French girl distracted her from even that.

THE THIRD DAY OF EDIE BERGER'S GLORIOUS REVOLUTION

The third day saw cats. Fifteen of them, to be precise, sunning themselves in the hall as though they had been there all along. Henry, who belonged to Mr. Richardson from the village[115] and had been smuggled back in Amelia Warren's jumper,[116] was stretched across the staff table; meanwhile Tabitha, who belonged to Mrs. White and had been lured back to the school by the promise of ear rubs from Sabia Gopal, was

. . . .

115   Mr. Richardson is a lovely chap. He is our local police officer and firefighter, all at once. It is a small village. We have to double up on such things. Luckily he does not get much call for either and so, instead, spends his days breeding delightful angora cats. Sometimes I wonder what he would do in an actual emergency.

116   Amelia and Sabia had decided to combine their trip to the dentist with some impromptu cat-wrangling. The only problem was that they had been discovered halfway through stuffing Princess Tibbles into their rucksack by Good Sister Paulette. Luckily Good Sister Paulette suffers from a rather acute case of blindness where cats are concerned. It is the most curious thing. She simply cannot see them. She did, however, insist that they charter a taxi back to the school and allowed Prince Marmaduke from number four, Agapanthus Way, to sit in the front.

happily scratching her claws on the back of the headmistress's chair.

The headmistress screamed when she saw them. This is not the sort of thing one should do when one sees a cat. But the headmistress was not only allergic to most types of animals[117] but also had a marked distaste for animals in the curriculum, or indeed anywhere in the school. And so she screamed and the natural consequence of this was that the entire school came to see what she was screaming about.

As she stood there, Maisie Holloway had the great idea to release a mouse into the room. It was not, as she pointed out in hushed whispers, an actual mouse but rather a small remote-controlled toy, and she would never risk the life of an actual mouse because she wasn't a monster. Some of her roommates disagreed with this, remembering the night she had eaten fish fingers with custard, and there was a fierce and heartfelt discussion before they remembered that the headmistress herself was standing only a few meters away and that perhaps arguing was something best saved for later. This untimely situation was resolved by Sethi Gopal,[118] who reminded them all of her own particular special talent and suggested that it might prove a useful distraction. And so a decision was made: Just as the headmistress paused for breath and the room was suddenly silent, Sethi Gopal fainted in a remarkably convincing fashion onto the floor.

As the girls shouted for help and nuns rushed toward Sethi,

117 Technically she was allergic to feathers, fur, and, I suspect, fun.
118 Sabia's twin; identical in all ways save academic.

Maisie sent her remote-controlled mouse down the center of the hall and toward Henry. Henry was not the smartest of cats, nor indeed the youngest, but the sight of a mouse heading straight at him made him feel like a kitten again. Within seconds he was leaping off the table and heading straight toward it. In the process, he knocked over several glasses, three plates, and the fruit bowl that Good Sister Honey insisted on leaving out as a Good Message for the children. The noise was horrendous: the headmistress started screaming again, Sabia started crying, and several cats who were already quite confused about the last fifteen minutes suddenly realized that they were in the same room as many of their mortal enemies and started fighting. Prince Marmaduke of Marmalade gave up on all of this nonsense and started to carefully climb the curtains.[119]

"GET THESE ANIMALS OUT OF THIS ROOM," said the headmistress.

Some of the first-years bustled forward to help. Unfortunately several of them stood on Sethi Gopal, who let out a loud yell and then remembered she was supposed to have fainted and so fainted again. Good Sister Robin began singing for some reason that nobody else understood, and several cats started fighting in and around the headmistress's legs. It was quite beautifully chaotic.

"Did you have anything to do with this?" said Hanna to Edie,

---

[119] Unfortunately he was a fairly solid young cat who had not climbed anything for a long time and so ended up ripping the curtains rather more than climbing them.

as they watched Sabia Gopal disentangle a long-haired Persian from the cutlery. "No," said Edie. She looked deeply and utterly content. "It's really a two-star effort at best. They could do better. I'll drop by their room tonight and offer some tips."

"I'll pretend I didn't hear that," said Good Sister Christine, who had accidentally-on-purpose picked an excellent vantage point at the back of the room. She turned around to look at Calla, who was standing next to them and hadn't said a word since the whole thing had started. "Calla, you're very quiet. Is everything all right?"

And by the look Calla gave her, she realized that it was not.

It was very much not.

AN UNEXPECTED GIFT

Good Sister Christine took Calla out of the hall and led her down the corridor. She paused outside one classroom, before shaking her head and propelling Calla into another.

Calla said, "I haven't heard from my mum."

"Were you expecting to?" Good Sister Christine gestured toward a stool. "Have a seat. You're in boarding school. She's in the Amazon. There was going to be a brief point of disconnect, surely?"

"She promised to call in. Once when she landed, and once when she hit base camp, and she's done neither. And I was fine when she missed the first, but now she's missed the second and I don't—I don't think I'm fine." Saying it out loud made it all more horrible somehow and Calla found her hands shaking. Not much, but just enough. Just enough to remind her that this was the longest she'd been apart from her mum in forever. She didn't like it. "I can't do six months if she doesn't call," she said. "I just—I need to know that she's okay."

Good Sister Christine leaned forward and grabbed Calla's hands, stilling them. "Hey," she said softly. "Your mum is

Elizabeth North, and meeting her was one of the most remarkable moments in my life. I saw her heal a duck's wing like something out of a fairy tale. She made it better because she knew how, because her brain *knew* things, and I wanted to know the sort of person who could do that. She made a thousand tiny miracles happen, each and every day, and she made me a better person. She hasn't phoned. Fine. But something might have happened. Not the sort of thing that you're thinking of, but something . . . dull. Boring. Her phone might have died. She might have lost it. If she's anything like the Elizabeth I remember, she might have even forgotten that she was meant to call. The excitement of it all. You know."

"She wouldn't forget me," said Calla.

"No," said Good Sister Christine, "I don't think she would. I'm sorry I said that." She looked thoughtful for a moment, before delving into one of her voluminous pockets and producing a small and battered notebook, which she presented to Calla with an air of reverence.

"I promised you a book when I first met you, so here we are. This is one of your mum's old notebooks."

Calla turned over the first page and read the first sentence: *This book belongs to Elizabeth North.*

And something very precise and beautiful came to life inside her heart.

READING SOMETHING
LONG FORGOTTEN

It is a most precious thing to be given something old, and the notebook was so beautifully old that Calla could not quite comprehend it. It was not as old as some of the most precious books in the library, but it was still old enough to feel as though it held secrets in every word. The paper was thin and fine in places, and tore if you held it too tight. The ink had bled and the staples that held it together were rusty and thick with age, and the book itself had a soft but most pronounced curl to it. But for Calla, that book was like gold because it was a connection to her mother. Reading it helped her survive several more days at the School of the Good Sisters and even though the pranks continued, Calla barely noticed them. She was happy to eat with a spoon one evening because every other type of cutlery had disappeared; she was fine when the headmistress banned any more trips down to the village because somehow the girls ended up bringing cats back with them;[120] and she barely noticed when every writing implement in the

---

120 Good Sister Paulette had offered the counterargument that "Perhaps the *cats* keep bringing the *girls* back," but it hadn't gone terribly well.

school was replaced with a carrot.[121] Calla had something that connected her to her mum and she would not let that go.

And so, on the mornings when she woke up too early and yet too late to go back to sleep, she distracted herself by reading the little notebook. She propped it up on her pillow, snuggled down underneath her blankets, and dreamily traced her words over her mum's writing from so long ago. Elizabeth had been writing about the Amazon even then. She had made notes in English and then some in a different language for some reason before returning back to English. Every now and then, she wouldn't write anything at all and instead drew a beautiful image of a small brown duck or some part of its anatomy. Calla loved every inch of it, even the strange and incomprehensible bits, and she did so in a way she could not quite understand. The notebook became the first thing she would mention when the others woke up.

"There's a map on page ten," she said when she heard Hanna moving. "At least, I think it's a map. A bit of it's in another language. It's beautiful. She's been planning this trip all her life. It might even tell me exactly where she's gone."

Normally Hanna would have been very sympathetic toward this sort of thing, but she had an underground library to run. And so she said "Great" and jerked a thumb at the bags at the foot of her bed. "Come and help me with these? I have deliveries to make and Edie is off doing something with the sprinkler system."

Calla hadn't even noticed that Edie wasn't in the room. She

---

121 Beautiful, beautiful work, if I do say so myself.

nodded, sliding the notebook down into the hiding place she'd made for her phone before climbing out of bed. She padded over and tested one of the bags. "God, what do you have in here?"

"Books," said Hanna. She heaved a big *Woe is me but actually I am having the best time of my life* sigh. "I have deliveries to make. Sam Penrose wants a Faith Wilson, Heather Kirk wants a Judith Kerr, and Thea de Grazie wants the new KM Peyton and nobody is going to get anything unless I get these books out of here."

"But what about Good Sister Christine?"

"Staff meeting."

"At seven in the morning?"

Hanna rolled her eyes. "It's the latest idea of the headmistress. It's good for the mind. Apparently."

"It is *not*," said Calla, with deep and definite conviction. She grabbed one of the nearest bags and grimaced slightly before hefting it over her shoulder. "All right," she said. "I'm ready."

"Excellent," said Hanna. She propped their window open with a copy of *I Capture the Castle* and smiled at Calla. "Come on."

A NOTICE ON THE BULLETIN BOARD

Dear Girls,

In light of the continued malfeasance by certain parties, I see only one choice: a revision of the school rules. The following rules are now in session with immediate effect. Should you be found contravening any of them, you will face severe penalties. Think your choices through.

Signed,
Headmistress DeWitt, April 10th

1. *Girls shall remain in their own bedrooms after hours.*[122]
2. *No girl or member of staff shall leave the school without permission.*[123]
3. *If you are found on the roof, you will be expelled.*[124]
4. *Girls will practice silence during all communal meals.*[125]
5. *The optional spirulina smoothies for breakfast are now no longer optional.*[126]

---

122 Edie: "She wishes."
123 Edie: "Pointless."
124 Edie: "She won't find us."
125 Edie: "What is this even meant to mean?"
126 Edie: Silence. And then, thoughtfully, "I'm going to have to up my game."

A TELEPHONE CALL IS ANSWERED BY SOMEBODY UNEXPECTED

It was not that there was anything unusual about the concept of a Friday at the School of the Good Sisters, or that anything particularly unusual happened on the day itself. Edie woke up early to remove all the vowels from every computer keyboard in the school, and as Good Sister Christine was still caught up with extra staff meetings, Hanna had to go and deliver her books before the first bell and potential discovery. This meant that Calla was left all by herself in the North Tower bedroom and so she spent that time with her mother's notebook, and tried to ignore the fact that she had not yet heard from Elizabeth in person. The notebook was all very well and good (and oddly full of recipes for Victoria sponge) but it was not her mum.

And for some reason on that Friday, Calla's hand reached out to pick up her phone and dial her mum. She did not quite realize what she was doing until she was dialing the number.

The number for her mum's satellite phone was a long one, and it took a moment for her to check that all the numbers were in the right order. When it cut out almost straight away, she stared at it and wondered if she'd made a mistake. She rarely made mistakes with things she had memorized. Unlike Elizabeth, Calla always knew when the bills were due and just how long they could take before people got upset at them Not Paying Things. The number was right. She'd dialed it correctly. It was probably just her mum trying to remember how to work the phone.

Calla took a deep breath and dialed again.

And this time, somebody answered.

THANK YOU FOR YOUR CALL

"Hi there!" said a perky voice. "The individual you're calling—"

"Elizabeth North," said Elizabeth North.[127]

There was a brief pause, and then the other voice continued. ". . . has been kidnapped by one of our operatives. We're so sorry if this causes you any inconvenience! Now, you may be thinking about going to the police but we can assure you they cannot help. We can resolve this ourselves. Okay! So let's do that! Please press one to reply to a ransom note, press two to tell us that we won't get away with this, or press three to speak to a member of staff in person. Have a nice day!"

....

127   Her voice had been recorded and inserted into the message. You may
      have heard something similar if you have ever phoned and got some-
      body's voicemail. These really were very efficient kidnappers.

IN WHICH CALLA NORTH DOES NOT HAVE A NICE DAY

Calla realized several important things during the course of that phone call and, as you are not inside her head, nor inside mine, I shall help you out by putting these Important Things in bullet points. You might think this is because I have just discovered how to make bullet points on the computer and you would be right but that is beside the point. However, let's also consider this as an opportunity for you to be reminded of the three most important things you need to know right now:

- Calla's mother had been kidnapped.
- The police could not be involved.[128]
- It was up to Calla to rescue her.

---

128 Of course, Calla could have gone to the police. In fact, a little bit of me wishes she had, but I can understand why she didn't. Calla North was the sort of girl who was used to fixing problems herself before people arrived to ask questions.

TO THINK IS TO ACT

I am aware that you may not have had to rescue your mum from the clutches of kidnappers recently,[129] and because I am a helpful type, here are a few other facts that you ought to know before we go any further. Calla had spent her life rescuing her mother. Of course she had never rescued her from a kidnapping because they are not typical sorts of affairs that happen to people who mostly think about ducks, but she had rescued Elizabeth from a thousand other things. Burnt cakes, unpaid bills, and trying to pay the bus driver with a handful of sweets as opposed to actual currency. She had rescued Elizabeth from reading less than glowing school reports,[130] from having to participate in the parents' race,[131] and from

---

129 And if you have, really well done, you.

130 Between you and me, here is the truth about those reports. Calla accidentally-on-purpose lost them, and there you have it. Of course, Elizabeth should have noticed their absence but she has never been a particularly observant sort of person.

131 "Do you have sports day this year?" said Elizabeth.

"No we do not," said Calla, who had accidentally-on-purpose lost the letter home about that as well.

having to act as a chaperone on a school visit to the local museum.[132] If there was a problem in Elizabeth's life, Calla solved it. Sometimes she did this with tact, sometimes she did it with the subtlety of a brick, but she always did it.

And so she would solve this.

Calla North disentangled herself from the bedding and pulled some clothes on over her pajamas. She grabbed her mum's notebook and her phone off the floor and rammed them into her pockets,[133] before heading out of the North Tower bedroom.

Hanna was coming up the staircase as Calla marched down. She had the contented air of somebody who had delivered books before dawn and denied the oppressive regime another day of victory, and so she looked deeply surprised to see Calla out of her bed. If Hanna had learned anything during her time with Calla, it was that Calla was not a morning person, let alone a galloping-grimly-down-the-stairs sort of person.

"Where are you going?"

"To the head's study," said Calla.

Hanna's surprise turned to concern. It was the sort of concern that said *But why would you do such a thing are you really sure?* and normally, Calla would have paused to explain *Yes I am sure this is a good idea trust me* but she didn't have time and so she dodged Hanna and raced down the last few stairs. And then, when she hit the ground, she began to run.

---

132 Also accidentally-on-purpose lost. Sensing a theme?

133 Elizabeth was the sort of person who insisted on pockets being a feminist issue and sewing them into everything (even socks, which is less of a good idea than it seems).

She was going to rescue her mum. Elizabeth was going to come home, and even though Calla was somewhat unclear on the practicalities of how that might work, she was clear on one thing, at least: She would need help. Rescues were complicated things and she was in England and her mum was somewhere in the Amazon. Actually kidnapped. And to solve that, Calla would need an adult. An adult with money,[134] potentially some sort of flying thing, and a lot of biscuits.[135] An adult who was in charge.

And it was because of all these thoughts that Calla found herself banging on the door of the headmistress's study at seven a.m. that Friday morning.

134 For potential bribery/distracting the kidnappers by throwing coins at them/buying tea.
135 Biscuits should form part of every plan, naturally.

DISCOVERING THE TRUTH OF MAGDA DEWITT

"My mum's been kidnapped," said Calla, and because her heart was already flying across the Atlantic, she did not realize the terrible situation she had put herself in.

The headmistress was sitting at her desk, looking at some papers. She studied Calla with an odd expression. She did not seem surprised to see her, nor was she particularly upset about being disturbed at so early an hour. In fact, the headmistress was showing no emotion whatsoever and this, more than anything, should have told Calla that something was deeply wrong. Calla was, however, her mother's daughter and somewhat incapable of seeing what was happening right in front of her while possessed of a Great Idea. "I need to leave to go and rescue her. If we take a plane now, we can get to Manaus by tomorrow night. We can start looking for them there. Somebody will know something. They have to. My mum never goes anywhere without buying a lot of biscuits, so if we ask in all the shops . . ."

"I'm very fond of a fig roll, myself,"[136] said the headmistress,

---

136 Nobody normal says that, I can promise you.

reaching over the desk and picking up the receiver on her phone. She dialed a number and said, "Gareth, can you come to the study, please? Immediately. Thank you." She was smiling when she hung up and turned back to Calla. "How do you know that your mother has been kidnapped?"

"I rang her," said Calla. There was no point now in pretending that she didn't have a phone, so she took it from her pocket and placed it on the headmistress's desk as proof. "There was a weird message on her phone. It said that I couldn't call the police, and that she had been kidnapped."

The headmistress rested her head on her hands. "And what makes you think that Manaus is the best place to start the search? Wasn't your mother headed somewhere . . . else?"

"Yes," said Calla. She felt as if she might explode from tension. "But the kidnappers wouldn't have known where she was going, as she always kept it secret. Even from me. They must have gotten her in Manaus. She was starting there before going off to find this duck." She paused for breath before continuing. "But even if she got farther than Manaus, we can still find her. Save her, I mean. There's this book—Good Sister Christine gave it to me—and it's full of my mum's work. Drawings. And a map, too. I can't read all of the directions, but we can figure it out on the plane. It'll tell us where she is. There's time—but we have to go now."

The headmistress didn't move, but stared at Calla with a fierce, almost triumphant look on her face. "I need to know *exactly* where Elizabeth was headed," said the headmistress. "Show me this map of yours."

Calla rammed her hand in her pocket and pulled out the

notebook, placing it open on the desk. "There's a bit here where she goes on about pink wafers and she loves a pink wafer but they're not her favorite and then there's this bit that's in a language I don't understand but it mentions *Mallardus Amazonica*—"

The headmistress cut her off. "Calla, I speak sixteen languages.[137] This doesn't look like any of them. It has to be a code. Do you think you know your mother well enough to break it?"

"I don't know," said Calla. "I can try." She began to hop from one leg to another, unable to wait a moment longer. "Please, we have to get to Manaus—"

"How much do you know about this duck?"

"I know it's important, but that's it," said Calla, in the way that one might speak to somebody who really wasn't picking up on the fact that this was an emergency. "Look—it doesn't matter. We have to go *now*. Good Sister Honey has her pilot's license. She could fly us—"

"That duck is everything," said the headmistress. A curious light began to burn in her eyes. "*Mallardus Amazonica* is resistant to some of the worst illnesses in the world. It could carry a disease that might kill you and me, but the duck itself would be fine. People could use it—the whole world could be deliberately infected with something before anybody even thought of checking that little brown duck. Can you imagine

---

137 The headmistress could speak English, French, Spanish, Russian, Swedish, Esperanto, Polish, Czech, Arabic, Mandarin, Twi, Estonian, Dutch, Italian, Hungarian, and Klingon.

the power that gives somebody? Can you imagine how much we could sell this duck and this knowledge for, if we found it first? That's what we've wanted all along. And your mother is the only person standing in the way of us having that."

Calla stopped hopping.

She stopped breathing.

Us, she thought. *Us*.

IN WHICH A VILLAIN'S SPEECH IS MADE

"You," Calla said slowly. *"You."*

The headmistress nodded briskly. "I work for a company known as the Malus Organization.[138] We're the ones who kidnapped Elizabeth. We wanted her to tell us where to find *Mallardus Amazonica*. We've wanted that for a long time. But she was always more concerned with *studying* and *protecting* it than with how much money could be made from it. So we sent her off to the Amazon and when she arrived there, our Malus operatives were waiting for her."

Calla made a small, tight sound of worry. She said, "If you hurt her—"

"If only life were that simple," said the headmistress. "If our plan had worked, Elizabeth would have led us straight to the duck. But then—I don't know how—she figured out what was happening and managed to escape us. Did you know she could fly a plane?[139] She took one of our supply planes and managed to take off before we'd even noticed she'd gone. She disabled the

---

138 Sound familiar?

139 Calla had not, in fact, known this.

onboard tracking system[140] and we lost her somewhere over the rainforest. She's still there, somewhere under the canopy. We think she's gone to find *Mallardus Amazonica* and ensure its safety." The headmistress paused. "I rather hope she crashed."

"You won't find her," said Calla. "*Or* the duck. You've lost."

The headmistress smiled. "Oh, no," she said. "I haven't. Shall I tell you why?"

Calla didn't say anything, but the headmistress continued regardless. "Elizabeth didn't have time to pack. She may have a plane but she doesn't have anything else. No phone, no money, no luggage, and only enough food to last a week. Once she's eaten it, there's nothing left. No way to restock, not enough fuel to fly back to Manaus for help. So that leaves us with quite the pickle, doesn't it?"

"I don't understand," said Calla. "You can't—none of this makes sense."

"I am no liar," said the headmistress. "You can accuse me of a thousand things, but I do not lie. And so trust me when I tell you this: You will crack that code in your mother's notebooks and tell us where she is going, or she will die and that duck will remain undiscovered."

Calla stared at her with horror. "But what if I can't?"

"You will. And while you are working on that, we have a second plan: When Elizabeth looks up through the canopy, she'll see a plane pulling a banner behind it. Would you like to know what the message says?"

....

140 Good Sister Honey will be thrilled to know that her lessons on light aircraft maintenance have come in so handy, I can tell you.

Calla didn't answer. She couldn't. She had only just come to terms with the fact that her mother had been kidnapped. The fact that she now might be lost in the rainforest with only a week's worth of food was almost too much to handle.

"The banner says 'We Have Your Daughter.'" She smiled the sort of smile that made Calla feel sick and then very angry, all at once. "That's you, my dear girl. You were our insurance, but now you're also our hostage. Did you really think that I'd returned to this school because I *liked* it? No. I came here for you. You're the thing that's going to make your mother finally give up. When Elizabeth sees that banner, she'll send up a flare to reveal her location and then *Mallardus Amazonica* will be *mine*."

Calla found words from somewhere deep inside her heart. "She won't do that."

"She's your mother. She'll do anything to keep you safe."

"You don't know her."

"Frankly there are days when I wish I knew neither of you," said the headmistress.

"Was the letter from Belinda Freeman even real?" asked Calla.

"Belinda Freeman is one hundred and two years old," said the headmistress. "Of course the letter wasn't real."

Calla took a deep, steadying breath. "I'll shout for help. They'll hear me. There's an entire school out there. The nuns. The girls. They know where I am."

The headmistress shrugged. "Scream if you wish. The acoustics won't be in your favor. I cried myself to sleep for years in this school, and nobody ever heard a damn thing. If that experience taught me anything, Calla, it taught me how to be efficient. I have thought of everything you might want to do and I have put plans in against it. No girl in this building has access to a mobile phone. Nobody's allowed off-site without my knowledge. Nobody's going to help you."

"Edie will. And Hanna. Good Sister Christine. Good Sister June." Calla pulled the names to her as though she were in the sea and drowning. Everything was being taken away from her. There had to be something—*somebody*—she could hold on to.

"Good Sister Christine cannot leave the school and is terrified of challenging my authority," said the headmistress, folding down her fingers. "Edmée Berger and Hanna Kowalczyk are merely children, and Good Sister June is enjoying her forced retirement. There's nobody left, Calla."

And then, in response to this awful speech, Calla did the most curious thing.

She closed her eyes.

CALLA'S BRIEF AND WELL-TIMED FLASHBACK

Once, long ago, Elizabeth had taken her daughter to the fancy supermarket.

"We have money," she'd said, and that was all the explanation they needed. Money was something that did not come easily or often and when it did come, it was usually earmarked for a thousand other things rather than a trip to the fancy supermarket. Shoes. Clothes. Heating. Electricity. And sometimes not even those. Sometimes it was just enough for Elizabeth to catch the bus to the food bank and hope for the two of them to survive another day. But on this day, the money was enough to permit a trip to the fancy supermarket and the promise of anything in there for tea. And not just the reduced anythings.

Calla could barely contain her excitement and neither could Elizabeth. Both of them stood in the doorway and let themselves be dazzled by it. The brightness. The cleanliness.

"The dragon fruit," whispered Elizabeth, who had half thought she had dreamt this strange and marvelous thing from her childhood. "It's not actually a dragon, but anything that's got 'dragon' in its name has to be a little bit magic."

She could not stop herself from placing one of these in the basket, even though she could not really remember what to do with it.

A man at the end of the aisle looked up, locked eyes with Calla and Elizabeth, and started to walk toward them. For a moment, Calla grew confused and wondered if he was some sort of dragon-fruit guard. Perhaps you had to say a special word to him before you were allowed to have one. Perhaps every food in the fancy supermarket had a special guard and that was why it was all so fancy and expensive and the sort of thing that made her mum grow dreamy with longing.

"Boysenberry," said Elizabeth, who, of course, had not noticed any of this. Instead she had been staring at another section of the shelf and realizing that she had almost forgotten that there were other fruits in the world. They had spent weeks eating windfall apples given to them by Mrs. Merryweather from downstairs who knew more than she let on about Elizabeth's financial well-being. "I didn't even think these still existed."

"Mrs. North, isn't it?" said the man, arriving suddenly at Elizabeth's side. He was a tall man dressed in the sort of clothes that a shadow might wear. There was a peculiar logo on his blazer, like a duck with its wings crossed behind its back. Calla pulled at her mum's arm and when the man noticed this, he gave her a smile that was the very definition of a lie. "I'm talking to your mother," he said. "There's a car for you outside, Mrs. North. We can give you and Calla a lift home. All we ask is that you have a chat to us about your research. We're very interested to find out where you stand on a few matters of some urgency to our organization. You may have heard of us. We're the Malus Organization, and we'd love to—"

Elizabeth held up her hand. "Do you like boysenberries?"

"I don't—I don't . . . ," said the man. It was the first time that he looked as though he did not know what was going on. Calla rather liked it.

"Try one," said Elizabeth. "It's the law of soft fruit. You have to try one when you see it. Check the taste." She picked one up and ate it. Her eyes flared with a sudden, soft pleasure. "Try it."

The man looked at Calla again. Calla made an *Honestly, just try the berry, it'll be quicker* face. He made a *How on earth have you dealt with it this long?* face. Calla made a *She's my mum* face back at him, because that sort of explained everything and if he did not understand that then he really was the not very nice man that he appeared to be.

The man shrugged. "All right," he said. "But then you have to come with us."

Elizabeth leaned forward and carefully pushed one berry up each of his nostrils. "We're not going anywhere with you," she said.

DOING WHAT IS NOT EXPECTED OF YOU

The man had worked for the Malus Organization. And they had been trying to kidnap her mum, even then.

But instead of being kidnapped, Elizabeth had done the last thing that was expected of her.

Which was what Calla was going to do right now.[141]

"You're not keeping me anywhere," said Calla. The moment she finished speaking she lunged forward and grabbed the notebook from the headmistress's desk. She stuffed it into her pocket, pivoted, and reached out for the phone as well. And she would have reached it, had the enormous man not entered the study at that very moment.

"Where've you been?" the headmistress, who was turning bright red with rage, cried out. "Take this child to her bedroom!" She grabbed the phone and pulled it behind her, managing to move across the room quicker than Calla had ever thought possible. "And lock her in!"

Calla and the headmistress locked eyes.

"I was reading about ganache," said the enormous man in a

....

141 Unfortunately there were no berries on hand so, alas, this is all on a
    metaphorical level.

mildly offended sort of manner. "I know you've got me doing all this security, but I figured there wasn't much to do right now and my ganache does keep splitting."

"I don't care about your ruddy ganache," spat the headmistress. She reached out to grab Calla, who somehow managed to dodge her and in the process got closer to the study door. "GET THIS CHILD OUT OF HERE."

Calla could get herself out of there quite well and so she did. She took a deep breath and as the man said "Sorry, but I have to do what she says" and reached out for her, she threw herself forward toward the door. There was a complicated moment between the two of them where he had a hand on Calla's arm, but then she twisted and ran and left him holding her dressing gown sleeve. But not her.

Not her indeed.

Calla was halfway down the corridor by the time that either the headmistress or the enormous man realized what had happened. She ran past several of the other bedrooms full of contentedly snoring girls, past the hall and up a corridor that she'd never seen, before finding herself in an older part of the building full of stained glass and dusty old dried flowers. A part of her wanted to keep running but she found herself slowing down.

Elizabeth had escaped, and so would Calla. She just needed to take a moment to think things through and figure out what to do. Somehow, she needed to get in touch with people who would help her out, and not people who wanted to keep her hostage. People like the police. The fire service. The army. Maybe even NASA. Anybody. Everybody.

And so she ran.

AN INEVITABLE TRUTH

It is not easy to run around a building where at least two people are trying very hard to catch you, and it is even harder to find somewhere to hide in that building when it is full of girls and every nook and cranny is already occupied. Calla discovered this the moment that she turned a corner and ran straight into a queue of girls heading down for breakfast. The thought of breakfast reminded her that her mum didn't have enough food to stay hidden for long and made her stomach flutter with panic. She turned away and headed up the nearest corridor she could find, all the while keeping her head down and her eyes open for the arrival of the headmistress.

Calla knew she couldn't stay running forever. She knew she couldn't hide.

She had left her phone behind and she knew that the only other phone in the building was the landline in the headmistress's study.

So she had to go back.

But before Calla did that easily said and quite terrifying thing, she did something else. Something that, in fact, she had been longing to do ever since she had heard that message on the phone, only an hour earlier.

She had a tiny cry.

A tiny cry is this: You cry, and you let it happen, and then you pull yourself together. It is the sort of cry you have when you are determined to sort things out but are a little overwhelmed by the nature of everything you have been presented with.[142] And at that point in time, Calla was realizing all of this in the very sharp way that feelings sometimes make themselves felt. She pressed her back to the wall and scrubbed her hand over her face and tried to hold it all back, but it would not be held and so she had a tiny cry. She closed her eyes and sobbed into her sleeve and thought of sitting on the top stair with her mother and sharing the last biscuit between them, and even though it made her feel better to think of this, it strangely made her feel a little worse as well.

And all of this is why she did not notice the panel in the wall opening in front of her.

------

142 I, myself, have had a tiny cry upon being presented with a chocolate cake with jam in the middle when I was not expecting it. Of course, it does not parallel with Calla's situation, nor the life-and-death predicament faced by her mother in the Amazon, but then not much would.

THE OPPORTUNE ARRIVAL
OF EDMÉE BERGER

"*Salut*, Calla," said Edie, as though stepping out of a wall and finding her roommate crying in a deserted corridor was an everyday sort of occurrence. "What are you doing here? Shouldn't you be at breakfast? Is everything all right? Why on earth are you crying?"

Calla took a deep breath. "The headmistress is evil and kidnapped my mum but then she escaped into the rainforest and now the headmistress and this guy are trying to kidnap me to make my mum give herself up and—"

Edie held up her hand. "I think I've been waiting for this moment all my life." She gestured at the space she had just crawled out of. "One of the ways I get around the school unseen is by going through the tunnels. There is a whole maze of them behind the walls."

"What?" said Calla, staring at her. "What's that got to do with this?"

"Nobody knows about them but Hanna and myself,"[143] said

---

[143] I can assure you that at least some of the staff did know about the tunnels and used them to make trips down to the kitchens when they fancied a pink wafer in the middle of the night.

Edie. "I have been using them all this term. That is why *she* hasn't figured out who has been doing all the pranks. Also, it's how I've been able to get across the school without being seen."

"Oh," said Calla, who was rapidly starting to Figure Things Out.

"Come with me," said Edie.

GOING BEHIND THE WALLS

Going behind the walls may not be something that you are able to do in your house, as not many normal buildings offer the opportunity to do so. They tend to just have the one wall with a narrow space inside it stuffed with boring things like insulation and pipes and wiring, and then the outside. The School of the Good Sisters was not like that. It had been built in a haphazard fashion over the years with towers stuck on by people who liked towers, a kitchen added when people discovered they rather enjoyed hot meals, and bedrooms when people realized that the pupils did not enjoy sleeping in the broom cupboard. It is a building of circumstance and ambition, and one of the direct results of that ambition was the creation of a labyrinth of corridors between the walls. Some of them were the size of a very slender first-year and more cobweb than corridor, and others allowed three of the tallest girls to walk next to each other as though they were walking down the high street of Little Hampden itself. Some of the corridors led to panels that, if you worked them just right, could be lifted out from the wall to allow you to pass from one world into the next, whilst others had doors that looked like actual doors but when you opened them, led to nothing more than a long-abandoned mop.

And all of this had been half forgotten until the day that Edie Berger had discovered the tiny door hidden behind a bust of Good Sister Maria. A sliver of darkness where there should be no such thing. Cold air coming from a supposedly solid wall. A door that opened if you pushed it in a very particular manner. And when it did open, her heart almost exploded with joy. This was the sort of thing that made her heart whole and she did not look back from that day. What lay beyond that door was freedom, and freedom was something you did not easily find in a boarding school.

The space beyond the walls had become Edie's world and then, after a while, she had shared her secrets with Hanna, and now she had shared them with Calla, too. Of course, she had only done so after finishing her task[144] but then Edie has always been a professional when it comes to undermining disliked authority figures.

She waited until she was sure that the two of them were out of earshot before she began to question Calla. "You said something about a man? Is it that *grand* man? The one at Good Sister June's farewell dinner?"

Calla nodded. She tried to ignore the fact that there was a spider crawling up her leg. "He works for the headmistress

---

144 She had removed all the vowels from the computer keyboards, poured jelly into the headmistress's welly boots, and been observed lurking near the sprinkler system with a screwdriver and a suspicious look on her face.

and she works for something called the Malus Organization, which I don't know—?"

"It is a criminal organization. I follow them on Twitter." Edie helped Calla down a particularly steep step. "For professional reasons, obviously. Don't trip up here. We're just above the staff room and I guess they might notice if a foot comes through the ceiling. I am taking you somewhere safe, and then we will figure out what to do. Now, tell me *everything*. Why has your mother been kidnapped?"

So Calla took a deep breath and told Edie everything that she knew so far. Edie's face remained inscrutable throughout, although she did occasionally nod in a very knowing fashion.

"We need to call for help," Calla concluded. "Get people here. Somebody—anybody—there has to be—"

"The phone in that office is our first target," said Edie. "But *they'll* know that as much as we do. And I'll bet you anything that that man has been left to guard it. That means we'll have to get rid of him and—"

"My mum could be literally starving," said Calla. "We don't have time to waste. What about breaking out and going down to the village? I mean, I don't actually remember where it is, but there's a policeman down there and—"

"Not an option," said Edie. "The school is in lockdown." She balanced for a moment on the balls of her feet before turning right and heading up a narrow passage. "She's locked the front door, locked the back, and locked all of the windows, which are unbreakable on the lower floors. The fire escape is armed. I am attempting to disable this, but it is a work in progress. She did it all last night. I watched her from behind a statue of Good Sister Helena Constance. The only way we're getting out of this school is via the roof."

"I'm not jumping off a roof," Calla said as she followed Edie. She paused suddenly as a new smell hit her, one of bacon and eggs and the distant hint of something else that might be intended for lunch. All of a sudden she realized that she had not eaten since yesterday and her stomach let out a little noise of pain. "Are we by the kitchens now?" she said, trying to distract herself. Edie nodded. "But that's literally the other side of the building from the staff room. I don't understand how we've got here so quickly. How did you work out where all of this went? How long did it take you?"

"It is like any secret," Edie said calmly. "All you have to do is figure it out. For example, a long while ago I was walking past this very same spot and I figured out that this was a door." She ran her fingers lovingly across a dark wood panel, pressed in on something that Calla couldn't see, and a door sprang to life underneath her hands. It was the sort of thing that you or I would never have noticed in a thousand years, but then Edie was the sort of person who could see things that others could not. "When I first found this door, I was not very happy. I was new at the school and I did not like it. Not one bit. Being at school was not for me. The food was horrible. There were no macarons to be found anywhere. I mean, can you imagine? The horror."

Calla had never had a macaron in her life. She wasn't even sure what they were.

"I was depressed," said Edie. She did not look at Calla. "I ate these things that people said were good for me and they were all puddings. Sticky toffee, chocolate, treacle, and Yorkshire. How can a country live so much on puddings? It is so strange. I did not like it. The food. The people. The nuns. So I ran away."

"You what?" said Calla, unable to stop herself.

Edie shrugged. "Yes," she said, still not turning around. "I found the door behind Good Sister Maria and I thought that it might lead me outside, but it led me here instead. I stayed inside these walls for a week, Calla. I only left to steal food and go to the toilet and the shower. The one person who figured out that I was here was Good Sister June, and she did not make me leave, for she is not that sort of woman. She came and sat with me one evening and we talked about literature and patisseries. Let me tell you, the woman's knowledge of crème anglaise is unparalleled."

A part of Calla could not quite believe what she was hearing. "Why are you telling me this?"

Edie smiled and pushed the door open to reveal a large room full of books and sofas and possessing the sort of smell that made Calla realize that nobody had been inside it for a very long time. "Because this is where I stayed when I ran away, and it's where you're going to hide. I will make sure that you get food, and pillows to sleep on if you need them, but most of all I will bring you help. But you must give me time."

And because Calla had no other option, and because she

believed in her friend in a way she did not quite understand, and because she knew that Edie *was* a friend, an actual, proper, true and honest friend who had come out fighting for her when she was at her lowest, she said, "All right. I'll stay here. I'll give you time."

THE INEVITABLE CONSEQUENCE
OF HIDING

Edie shut the door behind her.

Calla listened to the sound of her friend disappearing quickly down the corridors and then, as silence fell about her, began to feel somewhat overwhelmed. She could almost see the headmistress and Gareth climbing through the walls to come and find her. Every creak sounded like the footsteps of somebody big and adult-shaped, and every breath she took seemed to be the loudest breath she had ever taken. And now, so strangely, the room was feeling small and tight about her and she had to fight a desperate urge to open the door and run, run as fast as she could.

She was, I will let you know, having what can only be described as a mild panic attack. It is entirely understandable considering the stress that she had been under that morning and the knowledge of what was happening to her mother, right now, lost in the rainforest with a rapidly dwindling supply of food. The thought of being without food hit Calla hard, for she had spent much of her life hovering about the reduced section in the supermarket and sometimes, on the darkest days when money had seemed a long-forgotten thing, watching her mother being given food parcels to help them get through another few short hours. The simplest of things: a biscuit to dunk in a mug of tea, a crumpet laden with butter, or a slice of cake with icing as thick as the sponge itself, had been so often distant in her life. And now her mother was all alone, without her. Without hope.

Calla felt a shiver begin in her toes as she realized all of this, and it was the sort of shiver that once begun could not be stopped. It moved from her toes to her legs, up past her knees and into her stomach, and it sat for a long while there, making it hard for her to think clearly or even breathe, and then all of a sudden it moved out and up into her throat and into her arms and down all the way to her hands. Her fingers began to shake and she could not stop them. It was as if her whole body had been taken over by somebody else and she did not know what to do, other than ram her hands inside her pockets[145] and sit on them and will them to be still. But sometimes anxiety is stronger than anything we can imagine it to be, and so, suddenly furious with how her body was not behaving, Calla bounced to her feet and started to walk around the room. It was not an easy thing to do, for her legs felt as though they had never walked in their life and her throat was full of a fear she could not yet understand or master, but she did it. One step after another. Slowly, steadily, she did it. And with every step her anxiety and her worries

---

145 Pockets. Incredibly useful things.

and her panic began to fade away; her legs returned to her, her stomach began to feel normal, and her hands stopped shaking.

And it was then that she remembered her mother's notebook.

A LIGHTNING BOLT IN THE DARK

Calla sat down on one of the sofas in the corner of the room, and took the notebook out of her pocket. It was such a small thing and yet, because it might tell her where her mum was, it was suddenly the most important thing in the world. The pages were full of Elizabeth's neat writing, and every now and then there was a drawing of something that Calla recognized from her mum's research. Auriculars.[146] Speculums.[147] Custard creams.[148] Elizabeth had been planning this trip to the Amazon all her life and reading about it was like having her in the room. The thought that Calla had almost given the notebook to the headmistress made her feel quite sick.

The notebook had to stay with Calla, and both of them had to stay safe.

Calla flicked past the pages she had already looked at, and let her eyes drift over the new bits. The little brown duck kept

---

146 This is the fancy word for a duck's cheeks.
147 This is the fancy word for the patch of bright color you sometimes see on a duck's wing.
148 This is the fancy word for a small, tasty, and often quite misunderstood biscuit.

reappearing, as did the sections that Calla had thought were written in a different language. The headmistress had said that it was written in code, and that actually seemed like it might be a possibility. She picked a paragraph and began to study it, staring so hard at the letters that her eyes almost ached with effort.

But then her eyes drifted farther up the page.

And this is what she saw.

WHAT CALLA READ

Hi, Magda. I know you're going to read this, so I'm going to start to write in code now so you can't see what I'm doing. You know, if you'd just asked me about it, I would have told you everything I know about ducks from the start. They're so interesting! I mean, did you know that there is a breed of duck on every continent apart from Antarctica? And that when a duck sleeps, they can sleep with one eye open to make sure they don't get attacked? But I'm getting distracted. What I really meant to say was: Dhe reiu noching he ek dhat iu oc impkr tance dut sue wicls pekd dee ks tu ying tcf igkre dt out.

"'Tu ying tcf igkre dt out,'" Calla said softly to herself. "What even is that? How has she done this?" She drew her finger down to the next line and continued reading, turning over from one page to the next.

That's my answer to question five for history. I'm going to stop writing in code and tell you some more about Mallardus Amazonica *because I know how much it interests you. And it should! It's a very special duck! One day I'm going to go and visit where it came from. I've been figuring it out and I think I know exactly where that is: Dou nued tc look dor au pocnt wheke d fues hw ater ric er me eks dalt, und ics surko und ed dy sumethi ng thct makks dt aumost im cossi ble tk det out. Sc k dhi nk uts c valkey, dear tue Ric Negko, dnd ius onc k dong wuy awcy frok deo ple-i us goc tk de, ouherw ise thc du ckd huve becn dis ckvered dy nuw-anc th eke's dnly oue pla ce ok dhe mup thct lo kks dike iu micht fik da nd u thcnk Ilk de aule tc flk dhe re fu om macaus. K dhink iu hac tk de sume- where, toc, wheke dhe fuowers blcom ak didnight-tuere's a notk a fuund ic Spakish an un olc book, and tuat's thc onlk dhing tuat maces senke. dhere's auso thus thikg dbout tue Eact ank aest Wund anc I'k dot suce k dnderstand tuat yec, buk d wull.*

There, I've told you absolutely everything I know. Now I'm off for some cake with Chrissie. Have fun breaking my code. If you really, truly want to read about ducks, you will. And if you decide you're really interested and not just trying to copy me, I'll tell you everything.

Calla picked a bit of the coded section at random, and read it out loud again, hoping that it would make sense:

"'Dou nued tc look dor au pocnt wheke d fues hw ater ric er me eks dalt, und ics surko und ed dy sumethi ng thct makks dt aumost im cossi ble tk det out.'"

It wasn't the easiest thing to say in the world, but there were certain words that did make sense. *Dou* was a word that sounded like it might be *you,* and if she ignored the break in *sumethi ng,* it almost looked like *something.*

There was a pattern underneath it all. Her mum had never done anything without there being a good reason behind it. Of course a lot of those reasons were only understandable to

Elizabeth herself, and perhaps not logical in the slightest to those who thought in a more conventional manner, but they had still been reasons nevertheless.

A little, soft sound of pain escaped Calla at this point. She missed Elizabeth so much that it hurt, and so she shut the book for a second and closed her eyes, and told herself that it would be okay. Edie would come back. They'd rescue her mum. Everything would be all right. It had to be. There was no other choice.

And then she did not tell herself anything else, because she was asleep and dreaming of ducks and rainforests and maps that almost, but not quite, made sense.

IN WHICH EDIE BERGER DELIVERS ON HER PROMISE

When Calla woke up, she did not know where she was or what was happening. Much of this was to do with the fact that she was in a room she did not recognize, and that the small and determined figure of Edie Berger was currently sitting on top of her. It was a lot to take in and I think Calla did remarkably well under the circumstances by not saying something Quite Rude into Edie's face. Instead she pushed her off and pulled herself upright so that she could rub the sleep out of her eyes.

And when she did this, she paused and stared at the room around them.

Which was absolutely full of girls.

Edie picked herself up off the floor and looked intensely smug at the expression on Calla's face. "I told you that I would bring you help, and so I have. You can thank me later for being so remarkable and following through on my promise in just five hours. Five! Only five! Truly I am a professional when it comes to this sort of thing. Also, I threatened that if anybody woke you they would have to be my servant for the next three years."

"You're amazing," said Calla. She looked around the room. Rose and Gajal and Amelia were playing a very quiet game of tic-tac-toe on the floor. Sethi, Sabia, and Maisie were sprawled over an ancient sofa in the other corner of the room talking to each other in soft undertones.

"Calla is now awake," Edie announced grandly. "You can talk normally. We won't be overheard here. Not unless Good Sister Robin decides to visit the western attics, and as that has not happened once in the past three years and in fact I am not quite sure she even remembers where they are, I think we are safe."

Hanna carefully made her way over from the corner of the room where she had been quite contentedly building a book fort. She poked Calla in the shoulder in the way that you can only poke somebody when they are one of your very best friends. "I brought you a sausage roll," she said. "Good Sister Honey's been stress-baking. There are literally hundreds tucked away in a cupboard on the third floor."

"Thank you," said Calla, and she poked Hanna in the shoulder in the way that you can only poke somebody when you are realizing that they are one of your very best friends.

"Enough of baked goods," said Edie. She gestured at the crowd of girls gathered around them and then, when they did not quite pay her the appropriate amount of attention, she clapped her hands together and bellowed, "ATTENTION!" When the last first-year had turned around to look at her, she smiled benevolently. "Thank you, *mes enfants*. So! Now that our sleeping Calla has stopped her snoring, and now that I have inducted you all in the ways of the rooms between the walls, here is what is going to happen next. We are going to get Calla into the headmistress's study so she can call for help and so rescue her dear mother who is hiding out in the rainforest from the evil organization that is running our school. A complex challenge for anybody, I suspect, but not for people like you and me. This is *our* school. It was never Magda DeWitt's. It is time to take it back."

THE GREAT IDEA OF HANNA KOWALCZYK

Edie waited until the girls had finished cheering before she continued. "There is, however, one problem. There is an enormous man guarding the study and he must be removed. He is three times as tall as myself, and almost as wide as the building itself. He is stronger than seven bears and as terrifying as a patisserie without its delicate and beautiful cakes. We must get rid of him. Some of you may die in the process. It will be a noble death. We will sing songs about your sacrifice for years to come."

One of the nervier first-years gasped before several others hushed her.

"Nobody's going to die," Hanna said in a calming fashion. "Other than maybe Edie herself." She took the opportunity to pass Calla a biscuit. "Math cupboard on the second floor," she said, explaining. "There's a stash of jammie dodgers."

"We should set off the fire alarm," said a small red-haired girl.[149]

---

149 Her name was Faith Reed and she was deeply overexcited about being part of this group.

"But then the headmistress shall just reset it," said Edie, pacing furiously. "And to do that, she will be in the study. Precisely where we do not wish her to be."

"Not if there's an actual fire," said Rose.

Edie sighed. "Fire may feature in this plan. But it does not yet. Not until we have no other choice. Does anybody else have some ideas that do not involve setting things alight?"

"I do," said Hanna.

THIRTEEN BRIGHT YELLOW WIGS

There are many things you can do in a boarding school, but disappear is not one of them. At least, it is not one of the things that you can do easily, particularly in large numbers. Cover stories must be developed, coconspirators bought with the promise of jelly-bean payoffs, and the teachers must be the sort of teachers who do not notice when a vast number of their class is missing. Good Sister Christine was, I admit, somebody whose silence could often be bought with the right kind of confectionary[150] but she was also the sort of person to notice when Calla, Edie, and Hanna were among the missing and to deduce from this that Something Was Happening.

It was because of this that she set her class (at least, what was left of it) to do silent reading, and went out to check on the inhabitants of the North Tower bedroom personally. She did not tell anybody what she was doing and when she walked past the front door of the school and noticed that it was locked, she did not tell anybody about that, either. Because

---

150 My current rates for silence are, just to let you know, two jammie dodgers and a slice of Victoria sponge.

on her way to the front door, she had noticed that the windows were all shut and that the other doors had been locked as well, and that all of the keys to these windows and doors were missing. And although that was unusual in itself, it did not become Particularly Unusual until she realized that the headmistress was not in her study and was instead marching along the corridors like a possessed thundercloud. Her footsteps could be heard two floors down, as could her voice, which was currently yelling at Gareth to "Look harder, she has to be *somewhere!*" It was not a pleasant picture, but it was one that told Good Sister Christine that something was quite definitely, particularly, spectacularly wrong.

Good Sister Christine was not surprised to find that there was nobody in the North Tower bedroom, and she was also not surprised to see that the small purple car that ferried pupils to and from Little Hampden was still parked outside, and that the helicopter was still being repaired.[151] From this she deduced that the missing girls had definitely not gone unexpectedly to the dentist and that they were, in fact, still somewhere inside the school. And so she looked: behind statues, in abandoned classrooms, and—quite bravely—in the long-forgotten broom cupboard on the first floor that now held more cobwebs than brooms. And she continued to look, until all of a sudden she came across the most curious sight of a crowd of girls carefully lowering themselves from the ceiling in the lower fifth's common room.

It was not the rappelling girls that bothered her, for any

---

151 We have a helicopter. Now seemed a good time to mention it.

physical activity is a good thing and rappelling really did look like a lot of fun. But the fact that all of them were dressed as Calla North was somewhat problematic. The girls all wore the same school uniform and had, from somewhere, managed to find bright yellow wigs. Some of the more enterprising girls had drawn freckles on their faces, reminiscent of the freckles on Calla's own cheeks[152] but of course, if you studied them closely, you realized that several of these girls had done so with more hope than ambition and in more than one case, the freckles were, in fact, brown sauce.

Good Sister Christine waited until the last girl had reached the floor and had unclipped herself from her rope, and the missing floorboard in the ceiling had been replaced by whoever was left up there, before she coughed in a polite *Gosh, could you please tell me what's going on?* manner.

Several of the girls shrieked. One of the more flighty first-years gasped.

The one who was nearest to Good Sister Christine waved as though this was an everyday scenario. "Hello, Good Sister Christine. The school is being run by an evil organization who are trying to hold Calla hostage—so we must break into the study to call for help." She paused for breath. "On another note, we also need you to leave fifteen macarons behind the statue of Good Sister Theresa tonight, so that we[153] can use them to power our fight against evil. Please could you also

---

152 Three in a row, in the precise outline of a mallard's tertial feather.
153 Nobody else but Edie was going to get anywhere near those macarons, let me tell you.

leave some charcuterie? Just a small tray. Maybe some olives as well. I am not fussed as to what type or color, but a few will do."

Good Sister Christine took a deep breath. "Edie, why are you all wearing wigs?"

"How did you know it was me?" said Edie, looking quite disappointed. "I have not even shown you my Calla walk yet."

"Calla?" said Good Sister Christine. "I see Sethi, Sabia, and Hanna, but I don't see you—?"

Calla stepped out from behind a particularly tall first-year and gave the nun a small, awkward wave. The vision of so many other girls dressed like her had left her a little bit embarrassed but this felt like the sort of moment that needed her input. "It's all true," she said. "There's no time to explain everything fully. But we *have* to get into that study."

Good Sister Christine took a deep breath. The situation in front of her made very little sense, but she had no doubt whatsoever that the headmistress worked for an evil organization. This was not the sort of thing that she suspected of many people, but it fit the persona of the headmistress so well and explained so many of the strange things that had happened since the start of that term, she was rather disappointed she had not realized this sooner. Besides, she knew that Edie and Calla were not lying. She had witnessed Edie telling untruths and the rather remarkable fact that the greater the lie, the more innocent the small French girl looked. She rather suspected Calla was cut from a similar cloth.

And so Good Sister Christine came to a decision:[154] "Look, girls, whatever this is, I can't be involved officially, because I'll get fired within a heartbeat, but I'll help you out as much as I can. I'm with you." Several of the first-years, who were slightly giddy by this point, let out a very tiny cheer. Edie silenced them all with swift and strategic pokes in the arm.

Good Sister Christine ignored this side drama and crouched down so that she was talking directly to Calla. "Calla, are you all right?"

"I don't know," said Calla in a small voice. "But I will be. We just need to get into the study without the headmistress knowing."

Good Sister Christine nodded. "Say no more," she said. She straightened up, opened the common room door, and looked out into the corridor. "Were I the sort of person to have noticed other people in this room," she said, in a *just loud enough to catch the attention of everybody in the room but quiet enough to not attract outside attention* sort of manner, "I would be telling them that now might be a good time to go and do what they came here to do."

"Thank you," said Calla as she followed the other girls out of the room.

"Make me proud," said Good Sister Christine.

----

154 It was the right one, might I add.

IN WHICH BATTLE COMMENCES

The headmistress was not having a good day. It had begun well, with Calla presenting herself in the study like a turkey on Christmas Day, but it had gone rapidly downhill from that point. She had neither the girl nor her mother under her control and this did not sit comfortably with her. When she had also realized that a substantial number of girls had gone missing during the day, and that at least two of them were Edie and Hanna, and that Calla herself had to be somewhere but quite simply was not, she had gone from being uncomfortable to being angry. She had left Gareth to keep an eye on the study and spent the afternoon marching from one corridor to the next and willing herself not to explode with rage.

The problem was this: They needed Elizabeth. And now they did not have her. They needed Calla. And now they did not have her, either. This was no easy thing to deal with. Nor was the thought that, sooner or later, her employers were going to phone and ask her how the situation at the school was going. Gareth was good at answering the phone.

He was not good at coming up with convincing cover stories on the fly.[155]

It was only when the headmistress checked the fourth-floor laboratories for the third time that day that everything changed.

There was a small girl, a girl with hair the color of corn and a light sprinkling of freckles, sitting by herself in one of the classrooms.

The headmistress could not stop herself. She ran into the classroom and said, "Calla!"

And the girl gave her a grin. "You wish," she said, in an unexpectedly Polish accent, before suddenly—quite confusingly—being hoisted into the air and disappearing into the ceiling.

This, as you might imagine, was something that the headmistress had not expected to happen. She stood there for a moment doing a remarkable impression of somebody who could not quite believe what they were seeing[156] and then, upon hearing a burst of laughter outside the classroom door, she turned to see another girl standing there watching her.[157]

The girl looked just liked Calla.

And she was not—as far as the headmistress could see—attached to the ceiling and likely to disappear.

....

155 I am not quite sure what "on the fly" means, but I am assured by Edie that it is an appropriate expression to use at this point due to the poor state of Gareth's tradecraft. I am not even sure what "tradecraft" means, but sometimes it's better just to accept the truth of what Edie says and move on. If you don't, you're there all week.

156 It was no impression. She really didn't have a clue what was happening.

157 Rose Bastable, champion sprinter.

The headmistress ran to the door. She opened it and lunged for the girl, but she was already running down the corridor and the headmistress could not stop herself from following. The two of them hurtled around the corner before—quite suddenly—the girl that she had been chasing ran past another one on the stairs who looked just the same.

"What's going on?" said the headmistress, as she tried to understand what she was looking at. "What is this?"

The girl on the stairs smiled. "The most beautiful of things that could happen. The girls are rising against you. *Vive la resistance! Vive la revolution!*"[158]

The headmistress howled and lunged for her.

But the girls were already running.

---

158 Clearly, this one was Edie herself.

MEANWHILE, GARETH

Calla and Hanna were not aware of any of this, for they were at that moment having a discussion with the enormous man at the study door. Calla had been very nervous about going back to face him, but Hanna had persuaded her to do so.

"Sometimes it's important to face your fears head-on," she said, in the manner of somebody who had done this many more times than she liked to confess. "And we need to get to the phone in that study. We'll take some of the first-years and he won't be able to work out which one's you. I promise he won't. Adults aren't the quickest at working things out."[159]

Hanna proved to be quite accurate about the man's ability, or lack thereof, to distinguish between small children, even those he had grabbed at only a few hours before. He didn't figure out which one of them was Calla, not even when she stood right in front of him and asked to go into the study. It was as if they had never met.

"I can't," he said apologetically. "I have to mind this door and only go in if the phone rings. My boss—she's right particular

---

159 I confess she is not wrong.

about doing things her way, and things haven't been going the way they should. If she was here I'd ask her, but she's not. She's trying to find a girl."

"There are a lot of girls here," Hanna said wisely. "It is a girls' boarding school, after all. Was she after one in particular?"

Gareth shrugged. "Yep," he said. "But search me if I know why. She had yellow hair like you lot, and those freckles, too." He paused as he realized that he was surrounded by girls who matched that very description. "She's not one of you, is she?"

Calla shook her head. So did Hanna and the little crowd of first-years they'd taken with them. "Sorry," said one of the first-years. "We can tell you if we see her."

"But we don't know your name," said Hanna.

"Gareth,"[160] said the man. "I provide security where I'm wanted, and I've been wanted here this term. Honestly, I'd rather be baking. This job's been very dramatic, and a tiny little bit confusing. Some days I just long for a simple Victoria sponge."

"We *love* cake," one of the other first-years said dreamily. "We could talk about baking *forever*."

"Can I talk to you about ganache, then? I've been trying to make it, but it keeps splitting and I can't quite figure out why."

....

160 His name is Gareth Angus MacDonald to be precise, and I can tell you that he went on to become an excellent chef after all of this was done. I'm still in touch with him and sometimes he brings me cupcakes. His sister is called Helen Antonia MacDonald, which really, if you consider the initials of that, is a much more unfortunate state of affairs.

"Temperature," said the first first-year in a learned manner. "You have to get it just so, and not be afraid of—"

"Gareth, I'm sorry, but please will you open the study door for us?" said Hanna. She glared at the first first-year, the second first-year, and the other three first-years who were quite nervous but excited at being involved and had settled on saying nothing at all and just clutching each other breathlessly. "Gareth, please, it means a lot. We need to get to that phone and we're running out of time."

"I'm sorry, I can't," said Gareth. "Honestly, it'd be more than my job's worth. But I'm happy to talk to you. I mean—it's a bit difficult, though, with you all having the same color hair. And now, there's those other girls there."

Calla gave him a quick look. "Which other ones where?"

He gestured down the corridor. "Those other ones," he said, pointing at the group of yellow-haired girls that was running toward them.

The group of yellow-haired girls that was being chased by the headmistress.

THE DIPLOMATIC QUALITIES
OF GANACHE

Gareth shifted so that somehow he was blocking both the study door and any potential chance of an exit. "I'm sorry," he whispered to the first-years who were looking at him in a very accusatory sort of manner. "It's just that there's something clearly going on and I am meant to help her, and she does yell so awfully loudly. Look, I have to do my job, I'm sorry. Come and find me later so we can share recipes for sticky toffee pudding?" He paused and then, unable to stop himself, said, "I hear the secret is dates and I am *desperate* to try it."

One of the first-years nodded and was about to reply to him when Hanna bumped her with her hip and made a *Pay attention to what's going on* face. She jerked her thumb at the advancing group of girls and then back at Calla. They got the point and flocked in front of Calla, blocking her from view of the headmistress, whilst Gareth stood there and tried to figure out what was happening. When the other group of girls joined them, they did the same until Calla was surrounded by yellow wigs and freckles and people twice her height. To help matters even more, Calla brushed her hair forward so that it covered her face and stepped behind

Rose Bastable, who was the tallest in their year and twice the height of dear Good Sister Gwendolyn. Calla took a deep breath and tried to calm the wild fear inside her heart. Edie managed to position herself so that she was next to Calla and when she was there, she took Calla's hand in hers and squeezed it tight. And when Calla glanced at her, Edie smiled and winked.

Calla took a deep breath and looked straight at the face of the headmistress who was, I think, enjoying the moment a little bit too much. Actually, now that I have written that, I think I am being generous. The headmistress was enjoying herself in a manner that had made every girl there realize precisely just how evil she was.

"Well," she said, "you thought you were clever, didn't you? Setting me up all those traps. But here we are. Lambs to the slaughter."

Calla felt the headmistress look at her for what felt like forever before, suddenly, her gaze moved on to study the tall first-year at her side. A small voice inside Calla's head whispered: *She doesn't know which one you are.*

Gareth said, "I'm sorry, but there can't be any slaughtering— they've got tips for the perfect ganache and I need to figure out where I'm going wrong."

The headmistress stared at him as though she could not quite believe the conversation she was about to have.[161] "Ganache?"

"It's a mixture of chocolate—"

....

161 She could not.

"Shut up," she said. "This is no time to be talking about baking." One of the first-years made a little sound of horror.

"I know she's here," said the headmistress. "And though I am interested in your sudden ability to procure all these wigs and paint freckles on your faces, I'm more interested in getting my hands on Calla North. I won't punish any of you if you hand her over. It's better for you all if you just hand her over right now."

Sethi Gopal grabbed Calla's left hand. Sabia Gopal grabbed her right. Faith Reed made a vague *Not going to happen* noise. Rose Bastable stared very firmly at the ceiling. Hanna smiled blandly at the headmistress. One of the nameless first-years started to whistle. Nobody moved an inch.

Until all of a sudden somebody said, "I'm Calla."

And stepped forward.

THE BEAUTIFUL SACRIFICE OF EDIE BERGER

"I'm Calla," said the girl again. She stuck her hand up. "Please, if I come with you, will you let the others go safely? I've been crying all morning about it."

"Yes, of course," said the headmistress. "Do come along with me. I'll try to make you feel better." She tried to smile but failed substantially, and instead delivered the sort of grimace that a snake might give to its supper.

"Wait a minute," Calla said urgently as she watched all of this happen. Nobody was going to suffer for her. She had to deal with the headmistress herself. That's what her mum would do. She'd face up to this and try to solve the problem. "*I'm* Calla. I don't know who that is. She's pretending to be me."

The headmistress's eyes flicked from Calla to the other girl and then back again. It was clear that she still wasn't sure who was who. "Come with me, Calla," she said, talking to a space somewhere in between the two girls. "I'll speak to you other girls later. Gareth—take them back to their rooms. They need to take off those horrific wigs."

Calla stepped forward to follow the headmistress but then Hanna elbowed her forcefully in the ribs. "I'm Calla," she said, ignoring the fact that the real Calla was doubled up at her side and gasping for air. "The other two are lying. *I'm* the one you want."

"I know which girl I want," said the headmistress.[162]

"No you don't," said Sethi Gopal. "*I'm* Calla."

"No," said Rose Bastable, "I'm Calla. *I'm* the one you want."

"*I'm* Calla," said one of the first-years, rapturous with excitement. "Don't listen to them."

"Stop it, all of you," snapped the headmistress. She turned to glare at Gareth. "Aren't you meant to be working for me? Grab that girl."

He looked blankly back at her. "But which one, though? They're all called the same thing and they all look the same. It's a bit weird."

"You are looking for the child from this morning," the headmistress said through gritted teeth. Even from where she was standing, Calla could see the whiteness of her knuckles and the way she kept balling her fist. The headmistress was losing control of both the situation and herself. "The one that we have set up this entire thing for—the one whose mother we—"

"And then can I talk to them about ganache?"

The headmistress said a very rude word that I shall not repeat here.

Gareth took the hint. He made a *Sorry about this but it's the way it goes* face. "Look," he said. "I need the girl from this morning? I'm not sure which one you actually are, and I don't

---

162 She did not.

want to pick the wrong one, so it would be really helpful if you gave yourself up now? Would you mind? Please?"

Calla took a step forward, but she was already too late.

Because Edie Berger was a step ahead of her. "It is I," she said, thoroughly enjoying being the center of attention. "I am the one that you want." She smiled and held up her hands. "Handcuff me. Incarcerate me. Take me to the *Tuileries*."

And then, just as Gareth placed his hand on her shoulder and the headmistress opened the study door, Edie glanced back at the girls and her expression completely changed. "Run," she said urgently. "Run!"

LIVING TO FIGHT ANOTHER DAY

And so they did. At least, they tried to. The only problem was that several of the first-years were near tears over Edie's noble sacrifice for them, and Calla was starting to wonder if she'd even woken up and had been dreaming the entire thing, and so their run-away was more of a sort of *Let's all just move in the same direction and hope for the best* affair as opposed to anything purposeful and dynamic. It was a good job that Hanna was there or else I don't know what would have happened to them. She led the girls through one of secret doors that was tucked behind an umbrella stand in the math corridor, before bolting it shut behind them. For good measure, she pulled a plank of wood across the door as well.[163]

Nobody said anything until they got back to the hidden room. It was only then that Hanna finally cracked and had a tiny cry into the nearest cushion.

....

[163] You might be wondering where the plank of wood came from. I know I was when they told me this story, but then I decided not to ask anything else as it was almost lunchtime and Good Sister Honey was making some of her miraculous cheese and broccoli quiche.

"It's just that it's *Edie*," she explained when she felt sufficiently recovered. "She's been at my side since I *got* here, and she's done everything for me, ever, and now she's done this. She's sacrificed herself for us. She's in that woman's hands all by herself—!"

"She's our Gandalf," said one of the first-years in a swooning sort of fashion. "We'll write songs about her," said another first-year with misty eyes.

"I didn't want her to do it," Calla said tightly.

"It's Edie," said Hanna. "She was going to do it all along."

"But I didn't ask her to. I'll go back and hand myself in. This is all because of me. I hate the thought of her being with the headmistress all by herself. The woman's crazy. She tried to kidnap me."

"You're not going anywhere," said Rose, looking up from the packet of biscuits she had found under the sofa. Her expression was very serious despite the fact that her bright yellow wig was askew and several of her freckles had fallen off. "You can't think like that. We're your friends. We chose to do this, and Edie chose to hand herself over. She's bought us time. We have to figure out what we're going to do next. We have to get into that study." She pushed a biscuit over to Calla. "We're going to solve this. We'll get rid of that horrible woman and find your mum, I promise."

"Well, whatever we're going to do, we have to do it fast," said one of the first-years, eyeing the packet hungrily. "If the school's on lockdown, then that means we'll run out of food soon. I haven't had a biscuit for weeks now and I think I might actually die if that continues."

"The school's not the only thing that's going to run out of food," said Calla. "My mum doesn't have much time—"

Hanna grabbed the biscuits from Rose and pushed them at the first-year. "Eat," she said. "We'll never be short of biscuits in this school, trust me. There are custard creams in every cupboard." She paused suddenly and narrowed her eyes at the first-year. "Wait. Aren't you the first-year who was going on about ganache? What's your name?"

"Lucy," said the first-year. Her eyes grew wide at being noticed by one of her heroes. She tried to distract herself by nibbling at her biscuit but then her stomach realized what was happening and she accidentally-on-purpose devoured it in one bite. Being on the run from the authorities really was hungry work. Hanna graciously pretended not to notice all of this and handed her another biscuit. "Thank you," said Lucy. She blushed a little when she realized that everyone was looking at her. "It's just that my dad owns a bakery and sometimes he gets me to help him with it, and honestly ganache isn't that hard to do. I don't know why Gareth's having problems with it. I just forgot that we were doing, you know, what we were doing. Sorry, Calla."

"It's all right," said Calla.

"It's really not," said Hanna. "I don't know what we're going to do. We can't stay in here forever, not when Calla's mum's missing, and the school is being run by a madwoman, and Edie, our fearless leader, has been captured."

Calla grabbed her mum's notebook off the table and stuffed it into her pocket. She had the sneaking suspicion that she was having an Idea, and that it was the sort of Idea that meant they might not be hiding in the room between the walls for much longer. "Tell me about ganache," she said. "Lucy—please."

Hanna gave her a Look. "Did you hear any of what I just said?"

Lucy, on the other hand, looked thrilled. "Honestly, it's really useful," she began. "It can go into a thousand different things, like truffles and icing and sometimes, if you put it inside the middle of a cake and salt it, you can get salted ganache and—"

Calla held up her hand, stopping her. "Can you talk like that for about ten minutes?"

"Absolutely," said Lucy.

"Brilliant," said Calla. "Because I've got a plan."

A FURTHER FEW WORDS FROM YOUR NARRATOR

Adults sometimes like to pretend that they know everything.[164]

But Magda DeWitt had been the sort of child who frequently pretended to know everything, so it should be no surprise that she continued this pretense as a grown-up. But there were many things she did not know.

The headmistress did not, for example, know about the hidden doors that existed all across the school. And she had not considered the potential impact on her plans of a first-year skilled in the ways of ganache and a bodyguard who was quite keen to improve his cooking of such. She had not thought about the eyeholes in the painting that faced the study door and allowed people standing behind it to watch her coming and going. She had not remotely considered the fact that the girls might continue to fight even though their ringleader had been taken hostage.

And she had no idea of the enduring strength of Calla North.

....

164 They do not. Nobody, in fact, knows everything.

WHAT GARETH SAW NEXT

Gareth Angus MacDonald was having a crisis of confidence.[165] He had taken the job at the school because his passions were not paying. His passions, as you may have gathered, involved baking and in particular the fine, delicate work of the patisserie. *Patisserie* is French for "very fancy and very small cakes" and Gareth was really very good at it and had started a shop that sold cakes that were as beautiful as dreams. The only problem was that he was quite a substantial and scary-looking man and so nobody had ever quite believed that he had done the baking himself. His business had suffered, and so he had had to close and go into the security business. Security paid very well. And he had been very happy with how things had gone until he had discovered that the girls he was being paid to guard were actually quite pleasant[166] and that for reasons he did not quite understand he would have to replace his lunchtime éclair with a stick of broccoli.

---

165 This, in case you don't know, is a fancy expression for having a bit of an emotional wobble.

166 He is being generous here because nobody is pleasant all the time, but we must forgive him. He was having a complicated few days.

It was because of all of this that he looked uncommonly thrilled to see Lucy creeping down the corridor toward him. He had felt awful since their previous encounter and so the first thing he said to her was, "I'm sorry." Of course after this he said several other things including "She's not here" and "It's okay," but "I'm sorry" was the most important part of it all because he truly was sorry and a little part of him was starting to wonder if the headmistress was completely right about this school. People who knew about ganache were never the sorts of people who needed grounding in their rooms, in his experience.

Lucy grinned at him. When she came closer, she said, "I'm sorry we had to run off earlier but she can't have Calla. We're trying to look after her. It's nothing to do with you. We just had to run. It wasn't personal."

"That makes sense," said Gareth, even though it really didn't. He pulled a confused yet slightly wistful face.[167] "Honestly, I'd rather be baking. I only do this because I have to. My baking doesn't pay enough. People don't believe I've made the crème pat, and then when I split my ganache—"

"That's because you've got your ratios wrong," said Lucy. She looked thoughtful. "I could show you how to make it better. But—not here. I mean, we'd have to go to the kitchens. You

---

167 Some people might have described this as more of a *smelling a fart* face, but those people are called Edie Berger and weren't there to see it so can't have any input on the matter. Lucy has described it as wistful but quite confused, and as I have met Gareth, I think this is a description we can all go with.

can't cook in a corridor. Good Sister Honey would have an absolute fit."

"She would," said Gareth, who understood a lot about the particularities of chefs. He looked at Lucy and then down the corridor. There was no sign of the headmistress anywhere, and her absence made him come to a swift decision. He could leave the study and come back before she'd even realized he was gone. And if his slightly scary employer called, then they'd just have to leave a message. "Come on," he said. "Will you show me how to fix it? If we go now?"

"Of course," said Lucy.

If he had known her better, he would have noticed how relieved she looked, but I do not think Gareth really saw anything at that point. His mind was full of petit fours and truffles and cheesecake, and I think he practically skipped as he led the way to the kitchens.

The moment that Gareth and Lucy turned the corner, Calla and Hanna snuck out from where they'd been hiding and watching the whole thing. "Ready?" said Calla, staring at the study door. Within seconds, they'd be inside and phoning for help and it would all be okay.

"Always," said Hanna.

And they walked into the study together.

INSIDE THE HEADMISTRESS'S STUDY

It was the first time that Hanna had been into the study since the headmistress had arrived. The shock of what had changed made her stand quite still and say, "You didn't tell me it was like this."

"I didn't know what it was like before," said Calla with some justification. But I do, and so I shall tell you. When Good Sister June had been headmistress, she had had one shelf completely dedicated to the sort of china that one might use for afternoon tea, and another completely devoted to cake stands with handles so that they could be carried from shelf to table without disturbing the cakes. Another shelf had been full of biscuit tins and tubs: The cookies lived in a tin that celebrated the queen's golden jubilee; the pink wafers could be found in a duck-shaped box donated by a former pupil,[168] and the Viennese whirls were packed into a small tub that had *With Love from Cleethorpes* written across the top of it.

The headmistress had removed all of this. The room felt empty and cold.

....

168 The donor's name rhymes with Schmelizabeth Schmorth.

She also had a pile of documents on the desk that had caught Calla's eye. As a rule, you should not look at other people's belongings or even their quite-suspicious-looking files, but when that person has recently tried to kidnap both you and your mother, you do have a slight excuse. It is because of that that Calla was making the most of the moment and had begun to flick through the papers.

"Look," she said, "it's a map of the Amazon. She's been trying to work out where my mum is." *And failing*, she thought with a smile of satisfaction. Everywhere the headmistress had highlighted on the map had an angry cross cut through it. Elizabeth was nowhere to be found.

Hanna came over to join her. "Maybe there's evidence," she said, rummaging through some of the papers. "Adults do like that sort of thing. They are very bad at believing things that are super obvious sometimes. Is there something we can show the police when they get here?"

"There's a list of calls to Manaus. I can take that, for starters," said Calla, folding up the piece of paper and stuffing it into her sock. "And look, Han, look at this—she's been buying a lot of stuff online. I don't even know how to say half of them, but they sound weird." And not good weird, she thought, not the good sort of weird at all. There was a list of things labeled *Toxins* and another of *Poisons*. These were never good words to read, and especially not when they were next to each other.

"Pocket it," advised Hanna, unaware that Calla was doing precisely that. "Take everything. Take it twice if it looks particularly dodgy." She stretched across the desk and pulled the old-fashioned phone over, checking to make sure it was plugged into the wall. "Good Sister June had a pink phone. She bought it because it reminded her of pink wafers."[169]

She paused and then checked that the phone was working. Between you and me, this was less of a technical test and more of a gesture to distract herself from the fact that she was trying very hard not to cry. Once she had regained control of herself, she turned back to Calla. "Dial. Add an extra nine at the beginning, otherwise it will think that you're trying to dial somebody internally. Old-people technology can be quite confusing."

"You are amazing," said Calla. She did not dial, not immediately. She put the phone down and gave Hanna a fierce *I'm going to pretend I didn't see you almost cry then but I want you to know I am totally here for you* hug. And when she had finished, she began to dial. The first number. The second.

And then the line went dead.

Calla looked up. The headmistress stood in the doorway, the cable for the phone dangling uselessly in her hand and Gareth hovering nervously behind her.

"Gareth," she said, "grab those children."

---

169 This is true.

THE FALL OF THE NORTH TOWER BEDROOM

Edie studied the new arrivals in the North Tower bedroom with the sort of expression one might use to study the arrival of a cold kale risotto. It was not a good, nor positive, nor even remotely polite expression. Eventually, she decided to speak: "Next time I sacrifice myself in order to buy you some more time, remind me to, you know—not?"

Calla picked herself up off the floor and tried to ignore the sound of the door locking behind her. "She caught us in the study—"

"And now you are here," said Edie calmly, "which means that we are all locked in this room, which is a problem I did not expect to face. I have, of course, already tested the windows and the door, and confirmed that they are locked. I suspect that, even if we were to work the door free in some fashion, then she will have stationed that enormous man at the bottom of the stairs. It is what I would have done. She will think along similar lines. She is good. But not that good. But! Enough of my talents, tell me of the outside world. I have been locked in here for days."

"An hour," said Calla. "It's been literally just an hour." She sat down on the edge of her bed and pulled out the notebook from her pocket.[170] They still had it. They still had a chance. And that, more than anything, made Calla smile. It wasn't over yet.

"Well, it has felt like absolute weeks," said Edie. "When you remove yourself from the field of play, everything seems so much longer. That is why, my friends, the generals of the past did not leave the battle until it was won. It was the error of an *ingénue*, but I am not one anymore. I am battle-hardened—"

I am afraid we must leave Edie to carry on this soliloquy herself, for something else was happening in that room. And that something was this: Calla was starting to figure out the code in her mother's notebook. When she had looked at it before, she had been afraid that she couldn't do it. But Calla knew her mother better than any other person in the world and—perhaps due to the fact that she was both desperately tired and desperately terrified for her—the words were starting to swim about on the page and re-form themselves in a way that almost, almost began to mean something.

In a flash, her mother's words to Magda came back to her: *If you truly want to read about ducks, you will.*

She could almost *hear* her mother saying it.

....

170 Gareth was not the sort of henchman who could grab somebody and search them at the same time. He had grabbed Calla in the study and held her at a distance. Gareth was, and indeed is, the sort of man who could not happily handle something unless it came in a pastry case or was wrapped in a chocolate shell. And so on the day that he carried Calla to the North Tower bedroom, he had not searched her and found the notebook. I, for one, am quite glad that he was remiss in his duties.

Calla blinked and looked at a sentence at random.

Sc k dhi nk uts c valkey, dear tue Ric Negko, dnd ius onc k dong wuy awcy frok deo ple—i us goc tk de, ouherw ise thc du ckd huve becn dis ckvered dy nuw—anc th eke's dnly oue pla ce ok dhe mup thct lo kks dike iu micht fik da nd u thcnk Ilk de aule tc flk dhe re fu om macaus.

And as she stared at it, she started to realize that there was a very familiar word in the middle of all of this gibberish. "I need a pen," she said suddenly. Hanna threw one across the room, barely pausing in her argument with Edie. Calla didn't pay them any attention. She just grabbed the pen and started to pick out some very familiar letters in the code:

Sc dhi nk uts c valkey, dear tue Ric Negko, dnd ius onc k dong wuy awcy frok deo ple—i us goc tk de, ouherw ise thc du ckd huve becn dis ckvered dy nuw—anc th eke's dnly oue pla ce ok dhe mup thct lo kks dike iu micht fik da nd u thcnk Ilk de aule tc flk dhe re fu om macaus.

Just in case you cannot see it, I shall help you.

The letters that Calla had spotted spelled out the word: *duck.*

Which was quite a familiar word indeed for Calla North.

THE RISE OF THE NORTH TOWER BEDROOM

Once Calla figured out that the word *duck* was repeated in the sentence, she started to realize that some of the words made sense. All you had to do was ignore the *duck* letters in them. *Valkey* was *valley, macaus* was *Manaus, Ric Negko* had to be the Rio Negro—the river that her mum had studied for years—and maybe the point where *duck* was written out in full was actually just the word *duck* itself. Hanna and Edie were too busy bickering for her to tell them about this, and so Calla just worked the code out by herself in the way that her mother had done, all those years ago when Magda had tried to steal her homework. For a moment, time in the School of the Good Sisters, and indeed in the Amazon rainforest itself, where Elizabeth was currently surviving on the bourbon creams she had kept in her sock for precisely this sort of emergency, stood still. The whole world was waiting for Calla North to solve the mystery of *Mallardus Amazonica*, and solve it she did.

For the second thing she did was put in spaces around all of the words that she thought she knew, so that the sentence now looked something like this:

dhink utsc valkey, deartue Ric Negko, dndiusonckdong-

wuyawcyfrok deople—iusgoctkde, ouherwise thc duck d huve becn disckvered dy nuw—anc theke's dnly oue place ok dhe mup thct lo kks dike iu micht fikdand u thcnk Ilk de aule tc flk dhe re fu om macaus.

And once she did that, she saw that the *d* from the *duck* always appeared as the first letter in the words she had made. It wasn't just the *d*—the *k* did the same thing. She only had a few words but the *k* was always the fourth letter in them. Maybe the *d* was the first letter of the word, and the *u* the second, the *c* the third, and the *k* the fourth—and maybe, they weren't the original letters in the word at all.

Calla carefully wrote out the sentence again. She kept the gaps that she'd made and started to rearrange the remaining letters so that the *k* would be the fourth letter in a word, and the *u* and the *c* would be the second and third. Then she rewrote the sentence again and put in a star where the letters from *duck* should have gone and letters for the words that she thought she knew:

*hink *ts * valley, *ear t*e Rio Negro, *ndi*son***ongw*y aw*y fro* *eople—i*sgo*t* *e, o*herwise th* duck *h *ve be*n discovered *y n*w—an* there's *nly o*e pla*e o* *he m*p th*t lo*ks *ike i* mi*ht fi* *and * th*nk Il* *e a*le t* fl* *here f*om manaus.*

"What are you up to?" said Hanna, who had grown increasingly intrigued by both Calla's silence and the fact that she had not participated in a much-needed squashing of Edie's ego. She got up from her bed and wandered over to where Calla sat, hunched over the notebook. "Don't tell me it's homework. How can it be homework?"

"It's not," Calla said carefully. She hadn't even taken her eyes off the page. "I'm solving my mum's code."

Hanna let out a tiny shriek of surprise. Edie's reaction, predictably, was much more under control. "Excellent," she said, as though she had planned Calla's moment of revelation all by herself.[171] She pulled her blanket up and closed her eyes. "Wake me up when you are done. I shall tell you the next part of this plan."

"You have another part of the plan?" Hanna said disbelievingly.

"No," said Edie, accepting the point. "But I have time to think of one."

Calla did not hear this exchange for she was thinking of a Christmas once, long ago, when all she and Elizabeth had had was barely enough money to keep the heating on, let alone cook a Christmas dinner. They had feasted instead on the sheer wonderfulness of a whole day spent not worrying about bills, and a quiche, sent up by old Mrs. Merryweather from downstairs who saw more than she let on, and spent the afternoon playing word games until Calla had fallen asleep in the arms of her mother. And the two of them had spent the night like that, fully dressed and curled up underneath a pile of blankets and coats and not thinking about the ice on their windows and the rooms with no light bulbs left in them, for they were together.

When dawn had come, and their room swam in a fine, silvery light, they had awoken and—unwilling to move from their cozy nest—Elizabeth stretched out and pulled a book

....

171 Perhaps she had. I have learned not to underestimate dear Edie.

to them and began to read to Calla from it. This book was a dictionary—a book full of words and the meanings of them—and although it was not the sort of book that you might have expected to be read on a perfect wintery morning, it was perfect for the two of them, for it meant that they could stay together for a moment longer and pretend that the outside world did not exist.

It also meant that Calla was the sort of person to whom words were a best and lifelong friend, and codes did not stand a chance against her.

Especially codes that had been invented by Elizabeth North.

THE FINDING OF ELIZABETH NORTH

You need to look for a point where a freshwater river meets salt, and it's surrounded by something that makes it almost impossible to get out. So I think it's a valley, near the Rio Negro, and it's one a long way away from people—it's got to be, otherwise the duck'd have been discovered by now—and there's only one place on the map that looks like it might fit and I think I'll be able to fly there from Manaus. I think it has to be somewhere, too, where the flowers bloom at midnight— there's a note that I found in Spanish in an old book and that's the only thing that makes sense. There's also this thing about the east and the west winds and I'm not sure I understand that yet, but I will.

BEING BRAVE

And once she had finished reading this out loud to Edie and Hanna, Calla held the notebook close to her heart and said, "I know what we need to do next."

Edie opened her eyes and studied Calla carefully. "What's your idea?"

"We have to contact Good Sister June. She said that she'd come if I sent a signal. And what sort of signals do people use when they're stranded? Smoke. *Fire*."

Hanna issued a surprisingly sensible response to this curious statement. "Calla," she said with all the tact she could muster, "I know you've had a bad day, but we are not setting anything on fire."

But Edie held up a hand. "Go on," she said.

"We get outside, and we set a fire on the roof," said Calla. "We put it on the highest part of the roof we can reach—make it safe and controllable so we don't burn down the school—but we make it big enough and high up enough that *everyone* will see it. We don't need a phone if we've got a fire on the roof. Good Sister June, the police, the fire department. Maybe even NASA.[172] They'll all see it."

....

172 This is perhaps a little bit ambitious, but it was quite an ambitious sort of moment.

Hanna grinned. "There's a barrel out on the roof still, did you know that? Good Sister Paulette used it in her welding master class the week before you got here[173] and when her helicopter maintenance elective got canceled, nobody ever brought it back inside. We can use that. That would keep it controlled. And I've done survival classes with Good Sister Paulette. I know how to start a fire and make it safe."

"You never told me," said Edie, looking surprised. She studied Hanna as if it was the first time she'd ever seen her. "Is that what those extra classes were?"

Hanna nodded. "My parents have dangerous jobs and wanted me to be taught how to survive under any circumstances." She was not wrong. Hanna did not like to boast about it, but she had grown up in wealthy diplomatic circles and had had a bodyguard ever since she was born, even when she had not quite known what a bodyguard was.[174] "I'll come and set the fire, Calla. I think you might accidentally burn the school down, so I'm going to stop that from happening."

"Oh," said Calla, who was a little bit overwhelmed at the sudden realization of what true friendship could feel like. She had only ever had Miranda Price as a friend before, and Miranda Price was the sort of person who would leave you to deal with things by yourself without a backward glance.

"And me," said Edie. "Never let it be said that a campaign

---

173 Why she felt she had to do this on the roof escaped me at the time, but I am quite glad in hindsight that she did.

174 She still has bodyguards now, even though much of the immediate danger to her has passed. Good Sister Robin is proficient in jiujitsu, and Good Sister Paulette has a peculiarly deep knowledge of poison darts.

against the oppressor started without a Berger at the head of it." She bounced up out of her bed and rummaged in the nearest cupboard. There was a series of productive bangs before she turned around holding a screwdriver and a hammer, and with the light of battle in her eyes. She looked to Calla and said, "Tell me what the plan is."

Calla raised her eyebrows, a little startled to find Edie looking to her for direction.

"You are in charge now," Edie said with a small, satisfied smile. "What do we need to do?"

And suddenly Calla realized that Edie was not asking her what to do but rather telling her that she was her friend, and that she would be with her for life. That both of them would. Hanna, Edie, and Calla. The three of them were best friends now and forever.

"Break open that window," said Calla. "We're going to finish this."

THE HIGHEST POINT OF THE SCHOOL OF THE GOOD SISTERS

A fire is a curious thing to make at the best of times. There are scientific principles behind it, and ideal circumstances to make it in, and I do not think that the top of a tower, in the wind and mild British drizzle, is particularly conducive to either. And by the time Edie managed to break the window lock and the three of them had gotten out onto the flat roof, it was also growing dark.

Calla stared up toward the distant top of North Tower. Just looking at it made her feel dizzy. Next to her, Hanna was having a slight attack of nerves. "It's not that I don't want to do it. Because I do. More than anything. But how are we even supposed to get up there?"

"Ah, my dear Hanna Banana," said Edie with a deeply satisfied air. "How you underestimate me. This is the sort of situation that I, with my so-special skill set was born for." And she produced, from somewhere about her person, a rope, knotted carefully at regular intervals and tied into a wide loop at one end. "*Regardez.* Admire my ability to throw the loop of this rope around the turret and make it secure. Calla and I shall climb up first, and then *ma petite* Hanna Cabana, you shall tie the barrel to the rope. We haul it up, and also you, *ma petite cochon d'Inde* Hanna, and then we pull the rope up as well so that nobody can follow us. And by nobody, I mean our delightful headmistress."

"You are brilliant," said Calla.

"I am French," said Edie. "And together, let us get to work, my dear Calla Koala. We have a tower to climb and a barrel and a Hanna to reunite on top of it."

Half an hour later, during which the rope swayed perilously and the barrel turned out to be much heavier than an empty barrel has any right to be, they were all on top of the roof of the North Tower.

It was like standing on the very top of the world. In the distance, beyond the dark mass of trees surrounding the school, the lights of the village twinkled on the horizon. Little Hampden. The police station. The fire station. The convent. All of them were so close.

"I hope they see us," said Calla. "They *have* to see us."

"They will," said Hanna. "And just think how mad the headmistress is going to be." She laughed nervously.

"Don't think about it," said Calla. "Just concentrate on getting the fire going. Leave the rest to us." She gave Hanna some of the practice exam papers that they'd been given for homework the day before everything in the world had gone wrong. It is perhaps unnecessary to tell you that no member of the North Tower bedroom had actually done these papers. "Edie, where's the nearest bedroom we can get to? Who's in it?"

"Lower South," Edie said without missing a beat. She gestured down and to the left, at a small window cut into the side of a wall that was thick with ivy. "It's Claire and Eloise Taylor. First-years. Twins."

"Take me to them," said Calla. Ordered, really. She was possessed of a confidence that filled her from her head to her toes. It was as if she had been waiting all her life for the chance to signal for help from the top of a tower.

Hanna stayed to make kindling out of the exam papers and carefully line the barrel with the twigs scattered across the roof of the tower, as Edie and Calla climbed back down and started to make their way toward Lower South Tower. It was clear that Edie was familiar with the roof; despite the rapidly darkening sky and the height that they were at, she moved as if she was just walking down the street. Calla, on the other hand, stumbled and tripped in a way that made me quite nervous when they both told me of this.[175] The two of them climbed over chimneys and weather vanes, pausing as a headmistress-shaped shadow passed a nearby window.

"Claire is the taller one," said Edie, once the shadow had passed. "She likes toffee. Eloise is more of a macaroni and cheese sort of person. She is probably going to be wearing pink. It's her favorite colour. Pink hair, pink pj's, pink pencil case. Although she does not call it pink; she calls it 'rose.' I am yet to understand why—"

"How do you even know the names of all the first-years?" said Calla, as they traversed a particularly narrow and nervous-making stretch of the roof. Talking kept Calla from

175 It's a good job I wasn't there to stop them because, I suspect, I would have been stopping them with all the authority I could muster.

imagining what might happen if she slipped. "You even know their clothes and their favorite foods?"

"I have my reasons," Edie said as she started to move again. She clambered down the side of a wall, pausing only to make sure that Calla was all right. When the two of them reached a flat part of the roof again, she took Calla's hand in hers and pulled her over to the window.

"Reasons?" said Calla.

Edie sighed. "Of course I know the names of the first-years. I know all of them. I check on them each and every day to make sure that they are okay and that they are not trying to run away as I did. I do not want that for anybody. My time in the room between the walls was perfect, but it was not right. Nobody should ever feel like they do not belong somewhere. So, I keep an eye on them. Of course, I don't let them know I do because I am excellent at subterfuge and skullduggery, but I do it all the same. It is my job. It is the right thing to do."

Calla stared at her. Every time she thought she understood Edie Berger, she realized she didn't. Not at all. She was remarkable. "Does anybody else know about this?"

"Nobody but you," said Edie. She knocked on the glass and shrugged. "But that is enough."

GOOD EVENING, ELOISE TAYLOR

"*Salut,* Eloise," said Edie, knocking on the window as though it were completely natural to make evening calls to each other across the rooftops.[176]

Eloise Taylor appeared at the window. She blinked. And then she stared at Edie in confusion.

"Open the window!" said Edie, helpfully miming precisely how to do this just in case Eloise had never come across the concept before. Eloise pointed to the lock in a *Well that's a very good mime but there is a lock in the way* sort of reply.

Edie rolled her eyes. "Must I do everything myself?" She produced the screwdriver and hammer and proceeded to break the lock open with her usual skill.

As they clambered into Lower South, Calla saw Claire slip out of the bedroom and disappear. Moments later she returned with the rest of the revolutionaries. Lucy, Amelia, Sethi, Sabia, Faith, Ellen, and Maisie. And behind them, pretty much the entire first year and a vast number of the second-years. By the time Edie had finished lecturing Eloise on the need to have an

....

176 It is not.

emergency toolkit on hand at *all times*, the room was full to the brim.

"Ah," said Edie, who had of course noticed this. "It is time for an inspiring speech. Claire, allow me your bed." Awe-struck, Claire stepped back and let the small French girl climb onto her bed. Once she was there, Edie cleared her throat in a dramatic fashion and lifted her hand.

Immediately, everybody looked at her.

Calla held her breath.

"My friends," said Edie, in the manner of somebody who has been delivering revolutionary speeches all her life. "I have a task for you and your numerous tiny associates. I—*we*—need your help. Calla and me. We would like a distraction of mag-nificent proportions, and I am asking you because I know you can do it. All of you must play havoc and let loose the dogs of war.[177] Do not look at me like that when I quote things at you! I pay attention to my English lessons. It is from an actual Shakespeare play! Not a very good one, but there we are, I pro-vide a quote and it must suit you. Look, my friends, it is not difficult. Please do not look at me as if I am asking you to fly to the moon. I am just asking you to make a distraction. The big-gest one you can. The loudest, the longest, the most distract-ing distraction you can ever imagine. All of you. Now is the moment. We are getting rid of the headmistress. Make your apologies to the dear Good Sisters, but they will understand.

....

177 Edie had gotten this quote wrong but she will never admit it if you ask her. The actual quote is "Cry 'Havoc!' and let slip the dogs of war" and so Eloise and Co. are to be forgiven for looking a little baffled.

This is necessary. Tell your friends. Tell everyone you have ever met. And don't stop making mischief. Not until you hear from me or Calla or Hanna. Do you understand?"

The girls nodded in mute wonder. One of them looked as if she'd fallen in love.

"I'll take that as a yes," said Edie. "Now, Calla and I must return to our faithful friend Hanna who is currently on the tower of our bedroom. We have a beacon to keep alight."

Calla came to a sudden and definitive realization. She could not take Edie away from these girls. They needed her. This was her time. "No," she said softly. "This is where you should be. This is your revolution. You need to go and lead it."

Edie nodded. She squeezed Calla's hand very tightly and then let it go. "Until we meet again."

LIGHTING THE FIRE

Whilst all of this was happening, Hanna was halfway through making the best fire she had ever made. She had picked up bundles of the loose twigs that had fallen onto the roof, and stuffed them into the bottom of the barrel next to a revision paper titled: *Thirty-Three Sums About Sago*. A little part of her had been a bit upset about burning anything that involved words, but then she had told herself that these weren't real words—they were instruments of torture—and thus managed to make herself feel a lot better about the whole thing. She felt even better when she saw a flame take hold at the bottom of the barrel and slide all the way up into the night sky. They had a fire, it was safely contained, and nothing was in the process of burning down. Now all she had to do was wait for Edie and Calla to come back to the top of the North Tower and join her. And to Hanna's eternal credit, she only screamed a little with surprise when this happened.

"Hello," said Calla, full of delightful calm. "It's only me." She had one hand on the protruding turret, the other still clutching the rope. When Hanna came to terms with the fact that the face in the dark belonged to one of her best friends, she stopped shrieking and pulled her up the last little bit.

When Calla's feet hit something stable, she turned round and hauled the rope up after her. "Edie is leading the first-years into battle," she explained. "And also a lot of the second-years, and also I think maybe everyone she's ever met."

Hanna nodded in understanding. "I'm glad you came back."

"We just have to wait now," said Calla.

"Yes," said Hanna. "We wait."

But there is nothing worse than waiting. The two of them pressed close to each other, and Calla held the notebook up to the light of the fire so that she could work on the code some more. It was so clear to her now that, even with the replaced letters and broken spaces, she could figure out words as if they'd been there all along. *Valley. Enclosed. Fresh water. Migration. Breeding ground. Cavern.* Her mother had figured it out by herself, all those years ago, and suddenly Calla felt very proud of her. Elizabeth North had been right all along.

And then Calla did not think about her mother any more, for something quite peculiar was happening beneath her feet.

The School of the Good Sisters was revolting.

Every lamp in every bedroom had been switched on and the curtains pulled back so that the light burned into the darkness. Every girl in every bedroom began to run around the corridors, shouting and laughing and talking to each other. In one distant corner of the building the school band began to play, whilst the third-form science room shook to the sound of a series of carefully controlled explosions. Hanna clasped her hands together in joy when she saw a corridor flooded with green smoke and then—suddenly—even Calla cried out with excitement—a series of fireworks ricocheted their way out of a ground-floor window and up into the night sky. The moment that the window smashed, the noise trebled until suddenly the girls on the tower roof were surrounded in it and they were crying and laughing and shouting with joy.

And the thing that Calla yelled was this: "We're coming, Mum, we're coming!"

A BRIEF NOTE FROM YOUR NARRATOR

So. For the next part of this story to work, I must tell you what was going on inside the school. And as there is only one person who can accurately describe the scene inside the school at that moment, I am forced to pass narration of the next chapter over to her. I will rescue you as soon as I can, I promise.

INTRODUCING EDIE

Salut! I am Edmée Agathe Aurore Berger and I am here to talk about what was happening inside the school because only I, of course, know. Calla had returned to Hanna up on the roof and was working out that notebook of hers by the light of the fire, and I went inside to create mischief and havoc and live the night of my dreams. Oh, my friends, it was so perfect, and it was even more perfect than that because it was necessary. Chaos has such an appeal when it is wanted and needed and desired, and I was the perfect person to lead the charge.

Of course I was not alone in this charge. Dear Eloise and friends had spread the message and the nuns helped as much as they could for, you see, they hated the headmistress as much as we did. They had done so ever since she had gotten rid of Good Sister June, for Good Sister June was—and is—beloved by us all. But because they were *adultes* and so bound by boring grown-up rules and things like that, they had remained silent and done very little. Clearly, they were waiting for a genius like myself to lead them, and so I did.

Reader, it was glorious. As I walked through the school, past waterslides and foam parties, past Gareth, who had been called to stop the third-formers from putting jelly into all of the desks and balancing buckets of water on top of all of the doors, girls would pop out of the walls and give me updates and news of the headmistress's whereabouts. Eloise Taylor appeared behind the statue of Santa Teresa with jelly in her hair and the light of battle in her eyes. She paused only to inform me that the head-mistress was making her way up to the second-years' common room before running off down the corridor. I called after her, "Eloise Taylor, you are magnificent, almost as magnificent as I," and then I ducked to avoid the thunderous arrival of a group of first-years, all heading toward the figure of Good Sister Christine, who was standing in the middle of the corridor and handing out books and food to anybody who passed.

"Edie!" she said upon seeing me. "I take it you're not at the dentist, then." She grinned and passed a copy of *The Little White Horse* to some small child at her feet.

"I am not," I said, grabbing the last fondant fancy before a rabid first-year could take it for herself. "Am I supposed to be?"

"No," said the dear nun, as she gave away books with a happy smile on her face. "But that's what the headmistress said about the three of you. Am I to understand she lied to us?"

"Yes," I said, helping myself to the sponge fingers that Sethi Gopal was carrying past me. Good Sister Christine handed out a copy of *Ballet Shoes* and a packet of pink wafers to another girl as she walked by. "Hanna and Calla are on the roof, tending a signal fire in the hope of alerting others to our plight."

"The beacons are lit," whispered Good Sister Christine. She held a copy of *The Return of the King*, from The Lord of the

Rings, to her chest and looked quite emotional. "Gondor calls for aid."

Because I did not have a clue what this meant, I said, "I do not have a clue what this means," and picked up a slice of Victoria sponge before the unappreciative hands of Rose Bastable could reach it. "But you need not worry about such things!" I said as I tucked into the cake, in a very calming and soothing manner. "Everything is safe! This is all part of our plan! We are hoping that Good Sister June will come and help us get rid of the headmistress in time so that we can go to Brazil and discover the place where Calla's mother is hiding out after the evil organization that the headmistress works for tried to kidnap her. It is all under control!"

And when I said that, the expression on Good Sister Christine's face changed completely. "What's this about Calla's mum," she said, and her voice was Quite Different. "What did you say? Tell me again, Edie, and get straight to the point."

"It is all under control!" I said brightly, because I am nothing but helpful. "The headmistress works for an evil organization, as you know. This organization tried to kidnap Calla's mother, but Calla's mother escaped and is now in hiding and only we know where she is because of a notebook full of notes about ducks of all things, which was written in code, but Calla can break the code so we know where her mother is hiding, but the headmistress is trying to hold Calla hostage in order to find this location or get her mother to give herself up!" And because I was finding this encounter much harder work than I had expected, I felt the need to take a custard cream out of the book cupboard and eat it while Good Sister Christine came to terms with everything. Strictly between you and me, she did not do very well at this. Her face went red and then white and her eyes almost fell out of her head. It was quite remarkable, really.

But eventually she said, "Where is Calla now?"

"With Hanna," I said, "on the roof."

"Then that's where I need to be," Good Sister Christine said decidedly. Really, she is a most impressive woman when she comes to a decision. I see a little bit of me has rubbed off on her. The British do not decide to do the right thing without trying to do the wrong thing first, in my experience, and yet here Good Sister Christine was, making the right decision all by herself and the first time round.

ANOTHER BRIEF WORD FROM YOUR NARRATOR

GET TO THE POINT, EDIE.

IN WHICH EDIE GETS TO THE POINT

SO THEN SHE SAID, "EDIE YOU ARE SO BRILLIANT WILL YOU TAKE OVER HERE WHILE I GO TO THE ROOF" AND I SAID, "I AM BRILLIANT AND I WILL ALSO LOOK AFTER EVERYTHING" AND SHE SAID "OKAY I AM VERY COOL WITH ALL OF THAT" AND BECAUSE IT WAS QUITE NOISY AND WE BOTH HAD A LOT ON OUR MINDS AND ONE OF THE FIRST-YEARS WAS RUNNING PAST US WITH A HOSEPIPE AND A WILD LOOK IN HER EYES, NEITHER OF US NOTICED THAT SOMEBODY WHO HAD BEEN HIDING QUITE CLOSE BY HEARD ALL OF THIS.

WHAT THAT PERSON HEARD

All of it.

She balled her fists when she heard it, and she balled them so tightly that her fingernails cut into the palms of her hands and made them bleed. But she did not storm out from her hiding place, not immediately, not until the girls had gone and Good Sister Christine had departed to find more books and buns.

They thought that they'd kept an eye on her, that they'd been able to track her through the building and remain out of her control, but she knew at least some of the school's secrets. She did not know of the secrets between the walls, but she knew enough to shake a pack of overexcited girls who thought that she hadn't noticed them. She could have done it with her eyes closed.

When she heard Edie tell Good Sister Christine everything, the listener waited.

And then she headed up to the roof.

THE TYING UP OF LOOSE THREADS

And now we return to the two tenacious twelve-year-old girls on the roof and to the fire, which was burning its signal out into the sky as though its very life depended on it. I can tell you one thing: It had been seen. It had been seen by so many people.

But of course, they did not know that then. Hanna and Calla were simply standing there and watching as the school metaphorically exploded underneath their feet, and when they saw Good Sister Christine climb out of the North Tower bedroom window, it seemed only right to throw down the rope and help her climb to the top of the tower to join them. Once she had gotten her footing and come to terms with a fire in a barrel on the highest part of the school, Good Sister Christine hugged Calla and Hanna fiercely and said, "Next time you decide to do something like this, you should tell me."

"How did you know we were up here?" said Hanna, deciding to change the subject.

"Edie told me," said Good Sister Christine. "She's inside doing what she does best. I had to come out here. You shouldn't be on the roof without an adult. Just think if you'd have fallen off."

"We studied thermodynamics *and* astrology *and* welding out here every day last term," said Hanna with some offense. "Nobody fell off then, not even Good Sister Gwendolyn, and she's not the steadiest on her feet."

Calla decided to change the subject. "Did Edie tell you everything?"

Good Sister Christine nodded. "After a fashion. You've still got your mum's notebook?"

"Right here," said Calla. She waved it at the nun before stuffing it firmly back into her pocket. "I worked it out. My mum made a code and I can read it. There's a description of the duck's habitat and she's really specific. The type of plants. The type of water. The fact that it's close to Manaus and she thinks you can fly there, easily. There can't be many places that match that. We're going to find her, I know it."

A muffled explosion suddenly rocked the east wing of the school. A window cracked and green smoke began to thread out into the darkness. Good Sister Christine took a deep breath. "I have to get you to safety. If we could get to the car, I could take you away but Magda has the keys. That's not an option. We can't go down. So—" She fell silent as she tried to work out the options.

In the distance, Calla heard something that sounded very much like a helicopter taking off.[178] It felt like the sort of

---

178 It was a helicopter taking off, and it was to prove very important in the events that followed.

thing she needed to check with the others, and so she said, "Was that a helicopter taking off?"

"No," said Hanna, staring down at the North Tower bedroom window and the headmistress-shaped person who was currently climbing out of it. "It was company."

WHAT TO DO WITH UNINVITED GUESTS

One month ago, Calla had been at school with Miranda Price, hating every second of it. She had never thought that in a few weeks she would be standing on the top of a tower with a nun and one of her best friends. She had definitely never thought that she might be throwing balled-up exam papers at a head-mistress who wanted to keep her hostage in order to make her mum give up the location of a duck.

"If only we had water balloons," Hanna said as she launched *Fifty-Five Sums to Do with Kippers* at the headmistress's fore-head. It landed with a satisfying thud but, alas, on her knees.

"I am going to enroll you in throwing lessons next term," said Good Sister Christine. "Your aim is appalling. Calla, if it's you she wants, then you get behind me. She leaned forward and yelled, "You're not taking Calla. I won't let you. You'll have to take me instead."

"Don't be so ridiculous!" yelled the headmistress furiously. "Your brain isn't worth the effort, Chrissie. We all know that Elizabeth helped you get through school. The moment that *use-less* henchman of mine appears with a ladder, I am going to get him to climb that tower and bring me that child."

"I'm not going anywhere," Calla said grimly. She threw *Fourteen Recipes for Kale* at the headmistress, who promptly threw it right back at her. Luckily her aim was almost as bad as Hanna's, and the book sailed past Calla and squarely into the fire barrel. It burned up within minutes, sending a tall plume of orange fire straight up into the air. Calla turned to watch it, unable to stop herself, and then she noticed something very peculiar. There was a blue light coming up the road toward the school. The police. It had to be. The headmistress hadn't noticed.

Calla flung an exam paper (*Fifteen Sums to Do with Brussels Sprouts*) at the headmistress and said, "You're just using me to get to my mum because she won't give you the duck. IT'S JUST A DUCK."

"It is *not* just a duck," said the headmistress, with a dark smile. She rested her hands on her hips and stared at Calla. "There is something in that duck that means it can cure—or even *cause* illness. Just imagine how much money that could be worth. And the power! We could infect it with anything we want—and it wouldn't show the symptoms. Not one bit. But the moment it walked past somebody, they'd catch it and—within moments—infect everyone they meet. The people who find this duck will be the richest and most powerful in the world. Your mother is determined simply to *protect* it. But when she finds out we've got you, she'll have no choice but to give it to us."

Hanna let out a horrified gasp.

Good Sister Christine said something very rude.

Calla said, "That's never going to happen—"

And I am not sure what would have happened next between the four of them, were it not for the fact that at that very same moment, a very tall and substantial man stumbled through the North Tower bedroom window and onto the roof. This was Gareth, whom you have already met, and he was currently covered from top to toe in rainbow-colored foam.[179] He was Edie's last and greatest distraction, and although he did not realize it, he was about to change everything.

---

179 Edie had set off all of the sprinklers in the school, after doctoring the water with dish soap and food coloring. The foam was, as she has asked me to mention, nontoxic, non-flammable, and skin-friendly as "I'm not a monster."

WHAT GARETH DID NEXT

"Hello, Headmistress," Gareth said brightly. He wiped two little holes in the foam around his eyes so that he could see clearly and then, when he witnessed the curious situation before him, rather wished that he hadn't. "I'm sorry to interrupt whatever this is, but I thought you'd better know that I couldn't find a ladder and the girls have started to foam the school and honestly, it looks like fun and I don't want to chase them anymore, so do you mind if I don't?"

"I do," the headmistress said through gritted teeth as she dodged one of Good Sister Christine's shoes and a very angry glare from Calla. "Very much so. I want you to climb up that tower, with or without a ladder, and grab that girl."

"Right," said Gareth, who was growing more and more confused by the minute. "And honestly, I get that, but also, your visitors rang and said they'd be here in five minutes and you should have said you were expecting people, because I'd have made canapés. I know it's not part of my job description but I'd have quite liked it. I have this idea for a really good vol-au-vent and I've been dying to try it."

The headmistress froze. "Visitors?"

Good Sister Christine took off her other shoe.

Gareth paused in shaping the foam on his head into a unicorn horn. "Yes," he said, trying to look as serious as he could despite his appearance. "They rang and they'll be here shortly."

"But *who*?" said the headmistress, with the expression of somebody who has just been presented with a surprise exam. "I thought everything through. Ran a thousand scenarios. Not one of those involved people *visiting*. Who would visit this ridiculous school by choice?"

Good Sister Christine put down her shoe. Calla turned round to face her, ready to say something, but the nun simply placed her hand on her shoulder. It was the gesture of somebody who was in complete control. "This isn't a ridiculous school. It's the best place in the entire world. You could just never see it. Every single girl here matters. Every single girl here is going to change the world. That's why we teach things like baking and astrology and—helicopter maintenance."

Calla looked in the direction that the nun was pointing.

And saw a helicopter coming straight for them.

THE BENEFITS OF HELICOPTER MAINTENANCE

I suspect you might not ever have had a helicopter flying directly at you.[180] The headmistress had not, despite all of her criminal activities and nefarious work experience, and so she stood there and gaped as the helicopter came closer. Gareth also gaped but then he distracted himself by fashioning the foam on his head into two rather fetching horns.

"STAY WHERE YOU ARE," said somebody in the helicopter.[181] The noise had brought everyone in the school to the windows to watch and out of the corner of her eye, Calla spotted Edie at one of the top windows, surrounded by familiar faces. Sabia and Sethi Gopal. Rose Bastable. Eloise Taylor. All of them.

The headmistress stared at the helicopter.

"STEP AWAY FROM THE GIRLS AND ALSO THAT TERRIBLY

---

180 If you have, you have led Quite the Life.

181 Obviously, they were using a bullhorn from inside the helicopter to amplify their voice, for things were quite loud and they really did want to be heard very clearly at that point in time. It is a top tip for you to remember, should you be in similar circumstances. And, if you are, also bring a biscuit. Biscuits are excellent in a helicopter. The altitude gives them a certain bite.

GOOD NUN THAT IS UP THERE WITH THEM," said the voice. "DON'T YOU DARE CLIMB THAT TOWER."

"WHO IS THAT?" screamed the headmistress, who had never been good at dealing with a situation she was not completely in control of.

"IT'S ME," said the voice, and then when they realized that that wasn't very helpful when nobody could actually see them, they leaned out of the nearest window and waved.

And up at her window, a small French voice screamed with joy: "IT'S GOOD SISTER JUNE!"

RAPPELLING IS AN IMPORTANT SKILL

Calla had seen many things in her short life, a lot of them over the past twenty-four hours, but she had never seen a nun rappel from a helicopter. Good Sister June winched herself down onto the tower and, after unhooking herself, she checked on the fire and Hanna and Calla and Good Sister Christine in that order. "Everything all right?" she said, turning back to Calla once she had assured herself that everybody still had their limbs and the fire was under control. "I told you I'd come if you needed me. Just like I promised."

Calla made a *Have you noticed the horrible woman on the roof below us she is actually still a bit of a problem* face at the nun.

"She's not a problem," said Good Sister June. "You're being rescued." She began to hook Calla up to the rope she had winched herself down on, looping it carefully around her shoulders and then back to her waist. Once she had finished, she gave it a quick tug and turned round to say something to Good Sister Christine. Then before Calla quite realized what was happening, she was being hoisted into the air and pulled toward the helicopter and safety.

FLYING NUNS AND A VERY CONFUSED POLICE OFFICER

Of course Good Sister June did not leave Hanna or Good Sister Christine on the tower to face the wrath of the headmistress. She winched them up next, one after the other, into the helicopter that Good Sister Honey was keeping very still and steady. Once all three of them were safely in the helicopter, she plied them with chocolate wafers and told Good Sister Honey to land outside the front door of the school.

Good Sister Honey is a remarkable pilot under any circumstances and so she put the helicopter down precisely in the center of the school driveway, just to the left of the purple car and just in front of a very bemused-looking policeman.

The front door of the school opened and the headmistress ran down the stairs, closely followed by Gareth. The two of them carefully skirted the helicopter, even though the rotors were almost still by now, and went straight to the police officer. "Hello!" said the headmistress. A part of Calla could not quite believe how calm and in control she sounded. "Mr. Richardson! It's such a pleasure to see you, though I can't imagine why you've come—?"

A water balloon exploded at her feet.

"Well, there's a few things," Mr. Richardson said as he brushed cat hair off his coat and narrowed his eyes at the headmistress. "There's a fire on your roof, children stuck on a tower, and a girl at the window holding a THE HEADMISTRESS IS EVIL sign.[182] One of those things might be acceptable in isolation, but when you add something that looks a little bit like a riot that can be heard down in the village? That's the sort of thing that requires my attention and your explanation."

The headmistress shrugged. "High spirits," she said, ignoring the screams of disapproval from the girls inside the school and the Severe Looks from Good Sister June and her band of rescuees. "I've been taking charge of things and the girls have rebelled. It's a natural reaction to a firmer regime."

"You tried to kidnap my mum," said Calla. "You've spent the last twenty-four hours trying to kidnap me too. You IMPRISONED us!"

"It's true," chimed in Good Sister Christine.

"And she's been feeding us *kale*—" added Hanna, to whom this was clearly the worst of the headmistress's sins.

The headmistress made a *Well, you deserved it* face. "I'm just trying to do my job, Mr. Richardson, and I have a particular way of doing it."

Mr. Richardson glanced at Calla and then back at the headmistress. "It's a bit of a thing to be making up, surely? And then there's the word of the Good Sister here—"

"It's all true," said Good Sister Christine firmly. "These girls

....

182 Do I need to tell you that this was Edie? Really, she was ready for all situations.

were locked up in their room. She's been chasing them ever since they got out. She has plans—"

The headmistress laughed. "You don't have proof of anything," she said. "This is all made up. They're wasting your time."

But then somebody else spoke, and that somebody was Gareth. He had spent the last ten minutes trying to understand what was happening in the school, and when that effort had failed, he had paid attention to what was being said in front of him for perhaps the first time in his life. Dear Gareth is a complex individual, but he is no liar, nor does he run from what he has done. When he heard the headmistress tell her untruths about everything that had happened, he could not stop himself from saying, "But what about all of those papers you asked me to burn? And how you got me to lock up that girl? And how we tried to kidnap her mum in Brazil? What about that?" And when he had finished speaking, he felt the happiest he had felt for months. He walked over to Mr. Richardson and held out his hands helpfully. "I think you should arrest me. Honestly, I haven't felt right about any of this since I got here. I just wanted to be a decent security guard and make the occasional macaron."

"You can have a job here when you get out," said Good Sister June. "We can always find a place for a good chef."

"He is a *liar*," spat the headmistress. "There's no evidence for any of this."

It was perhaps unfortunate for her that that was the moment Calla remembered that the papers she had picked up in the study were still in her pocket. "But there is," she said, and she must be forgiven for taking an immense amount of pleasure in the moment. "It's in my pocket. A list of phone calls to Brazil plus a list of some of the things you bought online."

Mr. Richardson grinned at Calla and then, quite before the headmistress had realized what was happening, handcuffed her. "I'm arresting you on suspicion of false imprisonment," he said with some satisfaction. "And also attempted bodily harm, general nefarious deeds, and much more besides."

He looked at Good Sister June. "I assume you're able to step in again as headmistress?"

Good Sister June smiled. "It would be my absolute pleasure."

And that, as they say, was that.

A BLESSING OF NUNS

At least, that was almost that.

After Magda and Gareth were handcuffed and placed in the back of Mr. Richardson's car in a firm *Behave or else I'll set the first-years on you* sort of manner, the entire school streamed out of the front door to welcome back their beloved headmistress. You may not be surprised to know that it took quite some time for order to be restored and this was because nobody really wanted anything like that to happen. This was a party, and a party that has not been planned is the best sort of party in the entire world. Good Sister Honey produced a tray of freshly baked profiteroles, whilst Good Sister Robin led the school choir in several overexcited renditions of the school song, and some of the oldest girls began to let fireworks off on the roof under the careful eye of Good Sister Gwendolyn.

But Good Sister June saw none of this, for she was too busy watching Calla North. It was the look on her face that worried the nun the most. It was the same look that Elizabeth had given her all those years ago when she had told her that she had to give her dog away to

Mrs. Fraser.[183] It was a look that said that there was something else going on, and so Good Sister June walked over to where Calla stood and placed her hand on her shoulder.

"Calla," she said softly, "is there anything else you need to tell me? What don't I know?"

"My mum's in Brazil," said Calla. "They tried to kidnap her and now she's missing and I have to go for her. I have to bring her home. I have to go now."

"Of course you do," said Good Sister June.

And the simple honesty of her reply made Calla have a Tiny Cry of Relief.

"But," said Good Sister June, wrapping her arms around Calla and holding her close, "unless you've been taking a lot of extracurriculars this term that I'm unaware of, then you're nowhere near ready to fly a jet yourself.[184] A helicopter, maybe, but not a jet. So, that leaves us with a dilemma and that is this: Do you know what we call a group of nuns?"

Calla wiped her eyes and looked up at the nun. She had

183 You may be interested to know that once I finished writing this story, I sent a copy of it to each of the people mentioned within. One of those was Mrs. Fraser herself, who has now retired and spends her days sharing fondant fancies with a very elderly and intensely happy Aslan (who has special dog-friendly fondant fancies made especially for him). He has lived the most perfect and gentle of lives with her, and recently celebrated his twenty-second birthday.

184 This is a class that is restricted to girls in their final year of the school. This is not to say that the smaller girls cannot fly a plane, for they are certainly more than able. One should never doubt a tiny and purposeful girl. One should, however, be aware that sometimes her limbs are not quite long enough to reach all of the pedals.

expected Good Sister June to do a lot of things at this point, but not this. "You're . . . telling me a . . . joke?"

"A group of nuns is called a blessing," said Good Sister June. "And the staff of the School of the Good Sisters is more of a blessing than most. Good Sister Honey is both an excellent chef and former combat pilot. I imagine she could fly a plane whilst making a soufflé, and I suspect she probably has. Good Sister Christine is, as you know, the former childhood best friend of your mother and is one of the few people, other than myself and Elizabeth, to have seen *Mallardus Amazonica* in the wild. A relevant point, I think you'll admit. And then there's me, and I admit that I don't have any particularly special skills for rainforest navigation nor habitat identification but I am a headmistress.[185] Also, I *can* rappel from a helicopter in an emergency. So no, I am not telling you a joke. I am telling you that we are going to Brazil with you, Calla, and we're going to find your mother."

"We are coming too," said Edie, appearing out of nowhere with that remarkable skill of hers. She gave Good Sister June and Calla a wide grin. "I am told that Brazil does a custard tart which is *almost* as good as a macaron, and this is something I would very much like to try."

Hanna walked up to join them. "Also, I've read a *lot* of Eva Ibbotson and if you think I'm passing up the opportunity for a trip to the Amazon, you are super mistaken about that. It's practically part of my education."

Good Sister June nodded. These were both very good educational reasons, after all. "These are very good educational

185 And this, I feel is a superpower all of its own.

reasons," she said, and then she turned back to Calla. "Your mother is so strong," she said softly. "You need to realize that this isn't a rescue mission. Elizabeth has just got lost, Calla, as we all do, and we're going to find her. Together. And if you're ready, then we'll go right now."

Calla looked at them all. "I'm ready," she said.

Together, she thought, *together*.

ELIZABETH NORTH, SCIENTIST

It takes just over nineteen hours to fly from London to Manaus, which is more than enough time for me to tell you about what had happened to Elizabeth. The most important thing that you need to know is this: She was still alive.

But only just.

When Elizabeth realized that she had been kidnapped by the very people she had turned down before, the people who wanted *Mallardus Amazonica* for all the wrong reasons, her only thought had been to keep the duck safe. So she had, with a skill that had surprised even her,[186] managed to escape her kidnappers and steal their plane. She had gone deep into the rainforest with nothing but a backpack full of biscuits, which were enough rations for a week and no more, and flown toward the coordinates she had written down in her notebook all those years ago. Her plane had run out of fuel partway, and when a plane does that, they do tend to land. It is particularly fortunate that the trees in the Amazon are the

---

186 Although it was not a skill that surprised Good Sister Paulette, who had fond memories of Elizabeth's talents during her camouflage classes.

sort of trees that can cradle a light aircraft and make such a landing more of a landing than an actual crash.[187]

Once she had landed, Elizabeth had gotten out. She knew she could not stay with the plane for they would find that soon enough, and so she walked, and walked, and kept walking. She walked into the world that she had spent years longing to visit and she had been there ever since, looking for her duck and just trying to survive another day.

And after a while, something strange began to happen to her. She forgot the time, and the date, and in a way, she forgot herself a little bit as well. The rainforest was the kind of place where that sort of thing did not seem to matter, and so she did not let herself think of it. Instead, she rationed out her water and her food, and she studied the landscape she had spent her life dreaming about.

One day, she dreamed that she could hear people.[188] She knew that it was a dream because, even though she was awake, this

....

187 It is also particularly fortunate that a plane crash does help in finding somebody. It was one of the first things that Calla and her friends discovered and once they had the location of that, they were able to guess how far Elizabeth may have been able to walk from it, whilst cross-referencing those locations with the information that Calla had found in the notebook. There are not many places where the flowers bloom at midnight and the east and south winds meet above fresh water, and then it was only a question of hiring a guide to take them to see if one of them contained a forgetful and somewhat hungry scientist.

188 It was no dream. Hanna was finding the rainforest a lot to deal with. She had grown up in eastern Europe and knew woods and forests and trees. The landscape here was the same but so very different, and she was almost overwhelmed by it. Every step she took made her exclaim loudly in wonder.

world had seen nobody but her for years. Centuries, even. The tree canopy in this part of the forest was woven so tightly that nothing but the finest slits of light got through, and the undergrowth was so tall and thick that it came up to her waist. There was nobody here but her, and so the sounds of others meant that she was dreaming. There was no other option.

And she became even more convinced that she was dreaming when she saw a small girl with bright yellow hair and three freckles in the precise outline of a mallard's tertial feather, standing before her and holding a small brown duck in her arms.

The girl smiled at her and said, "*Mallardus Amazonica* migrates along the Marañón River, before working its way into the Amazon basin. After that, it reaches a nesting point somewhere up the Amazon River. Nobody knows where this nesting point is, but it has to be somewhere near to a valley and fresh water. It has to be somewhere so safe, and so distant from civilization, that nobody has ever found it. But people wrote about it—and somebody really smart worked it out. Back when she was a kid, she *knew*. She knew that it had to be where the flowers bloom at midnight, and the east and south winds can meet and twist into the sky as though they've been longing for each other all their lives. She knew that the birds didn't migrate, but every now and then—maybe once in a generation—a bird leaves to find a friend. The sort of friend that would spend their life trying to keep it safe."

And when her mother didn't move, a slow, teary smile crept across Calla's face. "It's you," she said. "Mum, it's you. The duck found *you* and even though it couldn't talk or tell you anything about it, you figured it out. You figured out where it came from and you kept it safe and you did that when you were just a kid. It found you. It found the one person in the entire world that would keep it safe." She was crying now, unable to stop herself. "And you—you found it and you kept it safe. And now, I've found you."

And at long last, Elizabeth understood.

She reached inside her pocket and produced something very small, very melted, and very precious. "I saved you a biscuit," she said.

ACKNOWLEDGMENTS

Thank you to my family for everything, always.

Thank you to Bryony Woods for your faith, appreciation of duck- and bun-based puns, and ability to spot a plot hole at a hundred paces. Thank you to Alli Hellegers for being a super-supportive voice in my corner. Thank you to Laura Godwin and all her team for helping the girls come to America and making the process all so lovely. And a very special thank you to Trisha Previte for designing, and to Flavia Sorrentino for illustrating this gorgeous cover. It makes my day every time I look at it.

Thank you to all of the bloggers, librarians, teachers, and booksellers out there who shout about children's literature each and every day. You're absolute stars.

Thank you to Francesca Arnavas, Alison Baker, Claire Boardman, Polly Faber, Matt Finch, acqueline Grant, Mélanie McGilloway, and Clara Vulliamy for being lovely and inspirational human beans.

Thank you to Alison Waller, Richard Walsh, Clémentine Beauvais, and Vanita Sundaram for helping me realize how much I enjoy a footnote.

Thank you to Angela Kroell, Elinor M. Brent-Dyer, Eva Ibbotson, and Phillipa Pearce for inspiring such eternally. And finally, thank you for reading.[1]